BLEED FOR ME

REVERIE HARGROVE

CHAPTER ONE

"Just a quick signature here… and you're all set." The lady sitting behind the desk flashes a big, white smile, and waves toward the waiting area. "You can wait for your turn there, One of the nurses will call your name once they're ready for you. In the meantime, may I fix a coffee for you? A tea, maybe?"

I blink at her, unsure of what to say. This place has nothing to do with the old blood center I used to frequent: the floor is clean, the air smells like hand sanitizer, and there are no junkies in sight. That coffee offer? Unbelievable. I'm used to non-existent queues, people yelling at you to hurry up or move out of the way, and unsanitary rooms. This feels like heaven. Well, it wasn't easy getting accepted here: they checked my blood—three times—I had to prove I didn't have any piercings or tattoos, and then I had to wait months before there was an opening for me. But it's worth it: for the same amount of blood I used to sell at my old blood center, the Health Bloodlife Clinic is going to pay me thrice as much. A chance I couldn't waste, given my situation.

"No, I'm good." I return her smile. "Thank you so much, though. It's very kind of you."

"Anything for our clients. Oh, before I forget", she adds, just as I'm about to turn around. "Welcome to HBC. We ly hope it will be a nice experience for you, Miss Deveraux."

It couldn't be otherwise, honestly.

I sit on a comfy, leathered armchair, and as I wait, I take the opportunity to work on my contemporary literature paper: it's due tomorrow and I'm still only halfway done. Okay, I haven't even started yet, but I've been busy.

C'mon, Coral. Five thousand words on the impact of feminism on postmodern American literature by tomorrow morning. You can totally do it.

I list a series of topics I want to cover and jot down a rough outline for my paper, but before I can start working on the actual first draft, my name gets called.

"Coral Deveraux?" A nurse wearing light green scrubs stands in the doorframe directly in front of me, eyes scanning the room. I'm the only one here, so she's quick to realize that Coral Deveraux is me. "Your turn, dear."

I quickly shove my notes into my backpack and jump up, following her into the sampling room. It's vastly different from what I'm used to: sunlight pours in from the big windows, painting lines of gold on the marble floor, on the white desk in the right corner, and on the cabinets lined against the walls.

"Make yourself comfortable" the nurse says as she sits on the swivel chair, already fiddling around with a sterilized needle. "Joanna Cartwright, your nurse for today. Nice to meet you."

"Coral." I wave awkwardly since she's not offering a hand for me to shake—it's probably for sanitary reasons. "Nice to meet you too."

"In your file it says you've asked for two whole units, today."

I lie down on the examination table, careful not to tear the clean strip of paper covering it, and I roll up the sleeve of my sweatshirt. "I have, yes."

She looks up from the empty syringe she's preparing for me. "That's a liter of blood, dear."

My smile becomes a bit forced; I can sense a lecture on the

way. "Yeah, I know."

It looks like she wants to say something else, maybe to try and convince me it's too much blood, but in the end she stays quiet. I appreciate it. I know damn well it's a lot of blood, just like I know I could end up feeling sick, but I have no choice.

The nurse draws all the blood in less than five minutes, quick and methodical, and after she's done, she applies a dotted plaster on the inside of my elbow.

"How are you feeling?" she asks, as she labels and stores all the vials with my blood in a small fridge.

Well, it's not *my* blood anymore: I've sold it and the clinic in turn will sell it for a much higher price. I wonder who's going to buy it: a high-end restaurant for vampires? A private customer? I'm never going to find out: HBC has a strict policy in terms of confidentiality, and I'm okay with it. I don't care who ends up drinking my blood as long as I get paid.

"I'm okay" I say, even though I'm starting to feel a bit lightheaded. "Thank you."

Once she's put away all the vials, she turns around and takes off her latex gloves, letting them fall into a small trash can. "We're all done here. Show Layla this," she hands me a freshly printed paper with my information on it, "and you'll get paid. Thank you for choosing HBC!"

I should be the one thanking them for choosing me, not the other way around, but my head is spinning too much. I'm only able to give her a shaky smile.

Before I can stumble out of the room, Joanna stops me to hand me something else. She places the small object on my palm and bends my fingers around it. "Here. Next time pick a single unit, dear, alright?"

As I walk toward the front desk, I open my hand. Sitting on my pale, sweaty palm, there's a strawberry candy, all nicely packaged in pink and cream plastic wrap.

Something tells me I'm definitely going to like it here.

CHAPTER TWO

By the time I park my rusty pickup in front of Cocoa and Pastries, the café where I've been working for the past three months, I'm still lightheaded. On the contrary, my wallet feels very heavy in my pocket: it's filled with ten crisp fifty-dollar bills that weren't in there before.

I finally get to pay my rent and stop worrying about ending up on the streets—there is nothing better, to be honest.

I walk into the café from the back entrance, but before I can even get to the changing room, the door slams open and Joseph pokes his head inside the staff-only area.

"There you are. I need you to wait tables, Amanda called in sick five minutes ago."

Classic Amanda. I wonder what's her excuse this time: the flu? Dysentery? Some bug devouring her from the inside?

"Alright" I sigh, forcing an unconvinced smile. "Five minutes and I'm out."

Working at Cocoa and Pastries isn't the worst: I like the place and the pay isn't half bad. Plus, whenever I close, I get to take home the leftovers that would otherwise be thrown away. It's a win-win situation. Still, it's not my dream job: the shifts are endless, the customers rude and the colleagues… well, let's just say Perpetually-Sick-Amanda is one of the best.

Today is pretty slow: there are few customers for most of

my shift, so I aimlessly stroll around the café and pretend to wipe already clean tables, trying to make myself look busy in front of Joseph.

I glance at the wall clock hanging behind the counter. Still half an hour to go and absolutely nothing to do. See, if Joseph were a decent guy, he'd let us kill time: I could study, read, fill in applications for new jobs. Joseph is anything but a decent guy, though, so we're forced to work even when there's no work to do.

The bells on the front door chime. I turn around in a heartbeat, eager for a distraction, but as soon as my eyes set on the newcomer, my enthusiasm quickly retracts.

The man entering the café with fast, nervous steps is none other than Ben J. Hamilton. He looks around, his big blue eyes scanning the room, and before I can react, he finds me.

"Coral." His smile is sheepish and a bit guilty, too. "Hey, I… I didn't know you'd be working today." He rubs his neck in a circular motion. "What a coincidence."

Coincidence my ass. I can't prove it, but I just know he has a printed copy of my schedule—maybe he even put it on his fridge with a Colosseum Magnet keeping it in place.

"I'll have someone take your order" I mumble, except there's nobody but me waiting tables today. Can I bribe the cook to do it?

Before I can turn around to hide in the kitchen and think of a plan, Ben grabs my wrist with his thick, sweaty fingers. "Can't you, like… do it yourself?"

For a second, I don't react: I feel his firm, demanding grip on me, his suffocating warmth hitting me in waves, his humid breath against my exposed forehead.

How I could I ever find his presence comforting?

I pull my arm free and open my mouth, ready to put him in his place, but I force myself to stop: Joseph is staring at us from the other side of the café, right behind the cash register. It seems like he's expecting a rage outburst from me, almost looking forward to it.

I close my mouth, letting out a shaky breath. "You can sit here" I snarl, my voice low and trembling, as I point at the closest table. "What would you like to order?"

He hesitates for a second, eyes lingering on me, then he sits down with a long sigh. "Just a coffee. You know how I take it, right? You haven't forgotten."

It's not a question, rather a firm statement. He's assuming I still know how he likes his coffee. He's not wrong: I remember everything, all those small, useless details I absorbed in the two and a half years we were together.

I would erase them all, if I only could; I would remove every single trace of him in a heartbeat. But sadly, I'm stuck with the memories, including the way he takes his stupid coffee. I could pretend not to remember—a petty tactic to show him he's not on my mind anymore, that he has no jurisdiction over my thoughts. But I don't want to be in his presence more than I strictly need to be, so I simply nod and back off toward the counter.

Ben likes his coffee diluted with half a cup of almond milk, two shots of caramel and some cinnamon dusted on top. It must be warm but not too much, and he wants it served with a teaspoon and a glass straw.

I set everything on a tray, adding napkins and sugar packets, but Ben is faster than me: he crosses the room with big, fast steps and takes a sit on a stool in front of the counter, a half-smile curving his mouth.

"I didn't want you to walk all the way there, so I came here instead."

I avoid pointing out it would be a matter of ten steps, and I give him a nod, busy pretending to clean an imaginary spot on the counter.

I can't believe he's here again. And pretending he didn't know I'd be working, too. It's simply ridiculous.

"Hey, Coral... can we please talk?"

There he goes. He's held back far too long for his standards.

"I told you last time, and the one before that" I say, turning my back to him. "I have nothing to tell you, and I'm not interested in whatever it is you have to say."

"Yes, alright, I get it. But if you could only—"

"No, Ben." I twirl around so fast my sight gets hazy and my head grows lighter for a second. I take a deep breath, fingers gripping the edge of the counter for a sense of stability. "No. It's over. You can't keep showing up everywhere I go, it's creepy!"

He leans in, eyes wide, his breath coming out in short and erratic huffs. "But you're not answering to my calls or messages! What else am I supposed to do?"

"Leave me alone" I articulate, holding his stare. "We're done, okay? I don't want to be with you, not anymore. Respect it."

"I'm not respecting shit, we're not done." He slams his fists on the counter, the glasses lined next to the slushie machine clinking together. "We're not fucking done. Not even close, Coral."

I take in a deep breath, only partially aware of Joseph's hard stare on me. As if this whole thing were my fault. "You can't force me to be with you."

My voice is weak, my words sound unconvinced, because deep down I know: he won't listen, he never does.

After throwing a couple of crumpled bills on the counter, though, Ben steps back, his eyes still digging a hole in my head.

My sigh of relief is pointless: he may be going away for now, but he will come back.

Of this, I'm sure.

CHAPTER THREE

"No, Coral, listen to me: he bothers you again, you go straight to the police."

It's been almost a week since the infamous day at Cocoa and Pastries, and I'm starting to regret telling my friends about it: they won't drop the subject, no matter how kindly I ask them.

"Nah, they won't do anything" Sasha says, walking fast despite her eyes being glued to the screen of her phone. "You could stab him."

"She can't just go around stabbing people" Piper points out. "Going to the police is the right thing to do, we all know it."

"Okay, alright, no stabbing." Sasha locks her phone and lets it slip in the back pocket of her baggy jeans. "What about a little blackmailing? A letter here, a message there…" In her eyes gleams a mischievous sparkle when she looks at me. "I bet he would stop harassing you."

Piper hits her pointy shoulder, stepping between us. "Absolutely not! Still illegal! Coral, please," she insists, turning her head to face me, "don't even think about it. It wouldn't end well."

"I think it would." Sasha leans forward, glancing at me from behind Piper's big, frizzy curls. "Let me know if you want to arrange something."

"Listen, you can't possibly be—"

Piper is unable to finish her sentence: in a matter of seconds, Sasha grabs her by the collar and forces her to bend down, their lips meeting in a kiss.

"Not… Not fair" Piper mumbles, her mouth still on Sasha's. "Shame on you."

"What, I can't even kiss my beautiful girlfriend now?"

My phone starts buzzing at the right moment: I love my friends and I love how much they're into each other, but the second they start being all lovey-dovey, I automatically become the third wheel. No, thanks.

The caller ID is unknown, but I answer nonetheless: anything to avoid my friends' cheesiness. "Hello?"

"Good evening" a posed, female voice says. "Is this Miss Deveraux?"

"It is. Who am I talking to?"

"It's Layla Finnegan" she answers drily. "We met at Health Bloodlife Clinic last week. Do you remember?"

"Oh, uhm…" I step backwards, clearing the path for a group walking toward the exit gates of Lehman University. "The lady at the front desk?"

"Correct. I'm sorry to bother you, Miss Deveraux, but…"

She hesitates for a second, long enough for me to assume the worst: is she trying to tell me I have a rare blood disease? That they can't sell my blood, so I need to give the money back? Well, good luck with that: those five hundred dollars are already in my landlord's pocket, barely covering last month's rent.

"There's been a situation" she sighs, a conflicted tone to her voice. "We need you to come here as soon as possible."

I stay quiet for a while, heart pounding in my chest. What kind of situation is she talking about? Is it the blood disease? Is it something far, far worse?

"Miss Deveraux, are you still with me?" she pushes.

I force myself to take a deep breath and nod, realizing

too late she can't see me. "Yes, I… I'm sorry, could you be more specific? What kind…" I inhale again, my eyes closed shut. "Am I sick?"

"Oh, dear! No, absolutely not, you're fine." A long sigh fills my phone. "I could have worded it in a different way, I apologize. You're neither sick nor in trouble."

I almost fall on my knees from relief. "Why are you calling, then?" I ask, my voice still a bit unsteady.

There's a moment of silence, before the lady speaks again. "It would be easier to explain it to you in person, I believe."

It seems weird, but I can't help being curious, and that's why I ask her when we can meet.

"Well… how quickly can you be here?"

CHAPTER FOUR

I had to skip lunch with my friends because the lady wouldn't stop harassing me, so by the time I park in front of the HBC building, I'm starving. I consider stopping at the pizza place across the street, but at last I decide against it: curiosity beats the hell out of hunger, apparently.

As soon as I pass through the clinic's door, the lady at the front desk—Layla, right?—jumps up and strides toward me in big steps, her face contorted into an expression that screams "uncomfortable but doing my best to hide it".

"Thank you for coming here on such short notice" she says, almost out of breath. "How are you?"

"I'm fine, but I don't think you should be the one asking questions" I point out, arching an eyebrow. "Why am I here?"

She quickly glances behind her back, suddenly tensing even more. "Well... There's been a situation."

"You've already said that. On the phone." I cross my arms, growing impatient. "What kind of situation are we talking about?"

She doesn't answer immediately: she looks down at her pointy, glimmering shoes, her shoulders trembling under the cream shirt. "You need to know that we tried to avoid it, Miss Deveraux. We tried to withhold the information from him, but… bu—"

"Avoid what?" I cut her off, my voice louder than I had expected. "And who is *him*?"

"I believe Miss Finnegan is referring to me."

My gaze shoots up, following the deep, rumbling sound of the voice. It belongs to the man standing in the middle of the lobby, occupying a space that not even two seconds ago was empty. Otherwise, I would have noticed him: he's not exactly the type of person who flies under the radar. Dark suit, black, slicked back hair, irises of midnight… in contrast, his skin is extremely pale.

I know the moment I meet his gaze: he's one of them. A vampire. But it doesn't make sense: they don't come out in broad daylight, never, not when doing so could lead them to their death. During the day vampires move across the city through underground passages, if they need to be somewhere, and usually the somewhere in question is a Night Building. The clinic definitely isn't.

Somebody could accuse me of lying, when I say this, but I'm not: I've never seen one of them. The places where I study, work, and hang out aren't popular among vampires. It's not like I do it on purpose, I'm not trying to avoid them as many people do: I'm not scared of vampires.

But right now, my firm belief is shaking.

"Hello, Miss Deveraux. It's nice meeting you, at last."

His voice is deep and runs like poison in my system, paralyzing me. I can barely think, and all I'm able to think about at the moment is the possibility to flee the clinic. The thought he couldn't follow me outside is comforting, and yet short-lasting: even now, he's standing in broad daylight. One ray of sunshine brushes over his forearms, exposed by his rolled-up sleeves. Running outside wouldn't make a difference.

"Is she mute?" he asks, turning his head to face Layla. "Or simply slow?"

She takes a deep, trembling breath, her eyes darting between the two of us. "Mr. Montgomery, I—"

"Neither" I cut her off. "But surely, you're very rude. Why am I here?"

"Miss Deveraux, as I told you on the phone, there's been—"

"I believe I'm more than capable of explaining the situation myself." Mr. Montgomery's voice is deep as a rumble of thunder.

I look at him. "Then do, please. I have a job. I can't waste my time like this."

He stares for a long moment, his eyes lazily searching my figure, taking me in one inch at a time. "Not here. This conversation shall remain private."

"I'm not following you anywhere" I tell him, moving backward. "And honestly, I'm not interested in what you have to say, so I'll get going now. See you never."

I can't even fully turn: the rude psycho *materializes* in front of me out of fucking thin air, a scowl on his pale face. "I wasn't done."

"Well, I am!" I shout, my heart pounding fast. "What... How! You know what, it doesn't matter. You can't force me to stay here and witness this creepy freakshow of yours!"

I try to walk past him, but once again, he gets in my way—this time with a very human step. "I won't dwell on your comments, Miss Deveraux, only for the sake of our meeting."

"Dwell all you want" I hiss, trying to get away from him, his presence large, uncomfortable. "This meeting is over."

"*Je n'ai besoin que d'un instant.*"

Once again, I end up paralyzed by this man's voice. No, he's no man: he may look like one, but in reality, he's a deadly, dangerous creature, capable of killing me without effort. I must remember that.

But he spoke French. I have no idea how he could

possibly know it's my first language, and a big part of me doesn't want to find out, but he still did. And I can't ignore that, not when it's been years since I've heard someone speak French.

I turn around, my legs unsteady and my breath a bit shaky. Not out of fear: this time, it's rage that's cursing through my veins. "So, let me get this straight: you gave him all my info for *what?*"

Layla's gaze struggles to hold mine. "Miss Deveraux, we didn't—"

"I thought you a had a strict policy when it came to privacy." I shake my head, unable to hide my disdain. "At least tell me why you did it."

Before Layla can answer, Mr. Montgomery steps in for the umpteenth time. "I've been trying, Miss Deveraux. You're making it more difficult than it needs to be."

I cannot believe my ears. "*I* am making it difficult? Are you kidding me?" I bark out a laugh. "Wow. You know what? Forget it. I'm out of here."

I get to reach the door before he speaks again.

"I have a job offer" he says, and his deep, smoky voice makes it sound like he's about to put forward an indecent proposal. "And if you wish to know more, you'll follow me somewhere private."

I hesitate. I don't know how, but he said exactly what I needed to hear in order to stop and listen. I have so many debts all the jobs in the world wouldn't be enough to pay them off, but I have to try somehow—I have to start somewhere. And I've been looking for a second job for months, now, to no avail. I can't run away without even listening to him.

"You can make your offer right here" I mumble, still giving him my back. "I don't see the problem."

"You know, Miss Deveraux." His voice is deep, rich and velvety—with a dangerous edge hidden behind the words. "If I wanted you dead, I wouldn't need to lure you elsewhere. Here would be perfectly fine." I feel him getting closer even though I don't see him. "I would bite into that pretty throat of yours and drain you dry in a matter of seconds. I would get away with it, too."

His words don't soothe my nerves, but he's right: he could kill me in a second, if he wanted to. I don't know about the getting-away-with-it part, but it's happened before, and the situation I'm in makes me think he's a powerful figure. He could probably bribe his way out of trouble. No, scratch that: I *know* he can.

I slowly turn around. He's gotten way closer than I thought: the point of his shoes rest inches from mine, and I can feel his warmth against my skin.

I still find it hard to believe that vampires are warm-blooded creatures. That they breathe, have a beating heart, can reproduce. They have something in common with their media counterparts, though: they are nearly immortal, can't usually stand in direct sunlight... and they're thirsty for human blood, of course.

"Miss Deveraux, I don't have all day."

His impatient tone calls me back to the present. I look around, throat clenching in anticipation, and I fill my lungs with a deep breath. "I swear, if you kill me, I'm going to be *so* pissed."

Yeah, that's my anxiety talking: it's responsible for my most inappropriate and questionable comebacks.

He doesn't say anything: after a dubious look in my direction, he turns and crosses the lobby as if he owned the place. He doesn't even look back to make sure I'm following: it's like he knows I won't back off at the very last minute—knows that I need another source of income as I need oxygen.

I follow him into the same room I was welcomed last time. Only, today there's no friendly nurse handing me candies to recover from a big blood draw. We're alone.

"Close the door for me."

"You know, saying please wouldn't kill you" I grumble, pushing the door shut with a powerful shove. "Just FYI."

Mr. Montgomery doesn't answer, and when I twirl around, I find him sitting behind the desk in the back. Wow, it really does look like he owns the place.

"I don't do pleasantries, Miss Deveraux" he finally says, a grim look in his eyes. "May I proceed?"

Turns out I was wrong before: we're not alone in here, his big ego fills up the room. There's barely any space left.

"Oh, please, do" I scoff, still beside the closed door. "I can't wait to hear why in the world you had that woman violate my privacy."

He's not amused. Quite the contrary, judging by his dark glower, but I don't let him intimidate me: I'm not the one in the wrong, here.

"My offer is quite simple." His long, pale fingers drum on the edge of the desk, following a steady and regular rhythm. "You let me feed directly off of you, I compensate your service with ten thousand dollars a month."

I stay still, feeling my eyes grow bigger and bigger. What? Did I hear him right?

"Wait, I don't think I understand" I stutter, rapidly blinking to try and wake up from what must be a dream of some sort. "What?"

"A remuneration of ten thousand dollars a month isn't enough?" he inquires, without batting an eye. "I will go higher, Miss Deveraux."

Holy crap, this can't be real. Is it some type of joke? A social experiment, perhaps?

I shake my head, trying to understand the situation. "So, you want to pay me to drink my blood."

He holds my stare, his face deadly serious. "Directly from you, yes."

I keep quiet for a long moment, then I burst out laughing. "I'm sorry, but... Is this a prank? It feels like a prank because..." A new, strong wave of laughter stops me from finishing the sentence. "Oh my god, *oh my god.*"

As I keep giggling, unable to stop myself, I can feel Mr. Montgomery staring at me with such intensity it burns my skin.

"I'm glad you find my proposition amusing, Miss Deveraux." But his voice almost sounds like a growl, so I wouldn't guarantee he's actually *that* glad.

"I'm sorry, it's just... You're not serious, are you?"

Mr. Montgomery slowly stands, his tall, sculpted frame dimming the light coming through the window behind him. "Do I look like the kind of individual who enjoys trifling?"

"You're right, my mistake. You seem funny like a wet sock."

I suppress my laughter altogether when he comes out from behind the desk, walking deliberately slow steps in my direction. He sure is big and menacing. God. Did I really have to provoke him? Was that necessary?

I retreat, trying to get away from him, but after three steps my back hits a wall. I have the urge to make myself small enough to disappear, but I keep my head high, watching him approach.

"You haven't answered my question" he says, his voice deep enough I can feel it vibrate all around me.

I give myself a few seconds to catch my breath, trying to put my thoughts together. "Wait a second... is this actually for real? I know, I know, you're allergic to jokes, we've verified it, but..."

"It's a simple question, Miss Deveraux" he insists, coming closer. "And so is the answer."

I can't help it: I start doing the math in my head. With ten thousand dollars a month, given I keep paying my other expenses with blood money and the weekly paycheck from the café, I could settle all my debts in a few months. And if I put aside a little something, after graduation I could immediately start to pay off my student loan.

Not half bad...

But still, this is out of discussion. Many would argue that selling my blood to the clinic isn't very different from this, but trust me, it is: what if he can't control himself? What if he ends up killing me? Not to mention he would have to *bite* me.

It feels like a punch in the stomach when I tell him, "The answer is no."

He doesn't drop his gaze, nor stops advancing. "Fifteen thousand."

I can feel my heart pound and my insides twist in protest as I shake my head. "You'll find someone else, Mr. Montgomery" I say. For a brief moment, I wonder what his first name is, but I quickly let the thought drift away. "I'm sure there's plenty of people willing to let you feed off of them for that amount of money."

"So naive" he murmurs, his voice a bit raspy as he keeps moving forward. "It's not about drinking right from any source. If it were the case, I'd simply contact a blood facility and have them send me a donor. I wouldn't even have to pay as much."

"Then I don't get what you want" I reply, my voice unsteady.

One more step and he's towering over me, his arms caging me against the wall. He leans in, slowly, one inch at a time, only stopping when his nose brushes against my neck. He's *sniffing* me.

"Your taste, Miss Deveraux." He moves back just enough to look me in the eyes. His gaze is dark and heavy on me. "Your taste forced me to inconvenience half the city to trace this clinic, and then you."

I hold his stare even though it's intimidating—it almost feels like he can read my thoughts. "So, you stalked me."

My answer catches him off guard, so I take the chance to slip away and power walk toward the door.

"I'm not interested" I say, even though it's not entirely true: part of me would do anything for that kind of money. "And don't bother raising your offer, because my answer won't change."

I give him one last look, and then I'm out.

See you never.

CHAPTER
FIVE

Later that night, I'm sitting on the beaten-up sofa in my apartment as I stare up at the ceiling. I can't do much else: at some point between this morning and the moment I came back home, the electricity company cut the power. How dare they! Okay, I haven't paid the bills in months, but still.

I couldn't even cook dinner: the microwave was inoperable, of course, so I had to eat stale crackers and two slices of expired ham. Gourmet, I know.

As I sit alone, the dark room flooded in blue light every two seconds by the blinking neon sign of the sketchy tattoo studio across the street, I can't stop thinking about Mr. Montgomery's offer. Jesus… If I had that kind of money, I wouldn't be eating expired ham, that's for sure.

But you don't, I tell myself, firmly shaking my head. *Stop thinking about it, Coral.* Ça suffit.

I can't. I've been trying for hours, during my shift at Cocoa and Pastries, while coming back home, and lastly as I was putting together my joke of a dinner, but my head just keeps going there.

It still feels surreal, the whole thing. How could this happen? My brain has tried to fill in the details I'm missing, such as why the clinic would give him my info. The only plausible explanation is that he paid them; he paid them to find out where the blood he clearly liked so much came from, but I can't quite wrap my head around it: it would be the same as me bribing someone at the grocery store to learn which chicken laid the eggs I bought last week, just because they were so delicious and I wanted that specific hen all to myself.

"Absolutely crazy" I whisper to myself. And while it *is* crazy, my thoughts still linger there. I wouldn't have to worry about bills, debts, food, or rent ever again. Well, until he got tired of me, anyway.

But no, it's out of question. I shouldn't even be thinking about it, let alone picturing my life with that kind of money on my hands. *Maman* is probably rolling in her grave right now: she was never particularly fond of vampires. The virus hit in the late 1800's, so we weren't there to witness it, but our ancestors were: they handed down stories about how at the beginning things were chaotic and violent and out of control, the very reason our lineage moved here from France at the beginning of the twentieth century. At the time, North America was a *safe* zone: you could run into the occasional vampire, but they mostly stayed in Europe and Asia.

Things changed, clearly. And while I know vampires aren't the uncontrolled savages my mother always described, warning me about their perpetual hunger, the mere thought of them still makes me a bit uneasy.

As I get up to collect the trash cluttering the coffee table, the doorbell rings three times. I glance in the direction of the wall clock; as soon as the neon sign across the street floods the room with blue, fluorescent light, I realize it's almost midnight—way too late for Sasha and Piper, my only usual visitors. It can't be my landlord, either: the rent has been paid and this month isn't due for another two weeks.

Another ring, longer this time. Then I hear a sigh. "Coral, baby, hi. It's me."

I freeze. The voice sounds thick and muffled, but I recognize it at once. It would be impossible not to. What is Ben doing here?

I stand still, holding my breath. I can hear his heavy, erratic footsteps stumbling outside my door, pacing back and forth.

"Open the door? Please? Kind of freezing out here."

It's freezing in here too, but I don't say it out loud.

I silently release a breath. I should have known something like this was bound to happen: the main door of this ratty apartment building doesn't close properly, so anyone can come in at any given time. Including Ben.

"Coral, c'mon." There's a hint of annoyance in his voice now. "I know you're in there. Open up."

Yeah, sure, because I'm completely stupid.

I keep quiet, a small part of me hoping it'll be enough to make him go away.

The doorbell starts ringing again, almost aggressively. It's so loud I bet the whole building can hear it.

"You can't ignore me forever" he growls over the constant ringing. "You can't, Coral. So, open this fucking door before I tear it down."

A loud thump follows his words, the weak wooden door vibrating.

"Go away *now*" I cry, my voice cracking. "We're no longer together, you moron, and even if we were… it wouldn't give you the right to talk to me like that!"

There's a moment of silence, then Ben starts banging on the door. Hard. "Open the fucking door!"

For a second, I can see it give in under the violence of his knocks. I'd lock myself in the bathroom, if the bathroom had a lock or even just a proper door. I doubt a bead curtain could keep me safe.

He wouldn't hurt me, right? I think. *He's only drunk and angry. He wouldn't do anything.*

But I'm not sure about that. I remember how he would punch walls and destroy things at any minor inconvenience, especially those last few months. It was one of the reasons I broke up with him: I felt unsafe, and love should never feel unsafe.

"You don't get to decide whether this is over or not." His voice is angry, a strangled cry. "It's not. You hear me, huh? We're still together, Coral, we'll be for as long as I please!"

More thumps, more rings from the doorbell, more cursing and screaming.

It goes on and on and on for what feels like an eternity, before I hear a key turning in its lock, muffled footsteps, and a female voice complaining about the noise.

I don't know who that is, but for a second I'm scared for her. Will Ben unleash his rage on this poor woman?

Just as I'm thinking about going out to help her, Ben murmurs something under his breath and slowly walks away.

I run to the window and look down. It takes him almost five minutes to come out the apartment building's door, head low and hands deep in his pockets. I don't look away until he's out of sight, then I let myself collapse onto the floor, a sob stuck in my throat.

Part of me hopes this will end soon, but deep down I know how unlikely it is.

What a nightmare.

CHAPTER SIX

It's a busy day at Cocoa & Pastries: the tables are all full, the air filled with chatter and a strong scent of coffee mixed with warm apple pie.

Amanda called in sick *again*—a strained ankle this time—so I'm replacing her for the umpteenth time. Luckily, I'm not alone: Geoff, the newcomer, is helping me.

"Take this one to table two" I say, giving him a tray with three fuming hot chocolates. "I need to clean the mess at table five. They broke a plate, the shards went everywhere."

"Table two. Gotcha."

I get the broom and dustpan from the storage room, and with my biggest, fakest smile, I make my way to table five. My thoughtfulness is unnecessary: the group of teens sitting here is too busy howling with laughter to notice my enthusiasm—or lack thereof.

I sweep the floor, throw away what's left of the plate and the pie, and lastly, I go back to the table and ask the group if I can bring them something else.

"Your number" laughs one of them, elbowing the boy sitting next to him.

Needless to say, they all snicker and praise him—some even high-five him.

I roll my eyes. "Yeah, not on the menu."

"What about you?" he insists, his gaze persistent. "Are you on the menu, sweetheart?"

More laughter, more eye-rolling on my part. "I'm not edible."

"I could still eat you. Bet you taste good."

His words remind me of what happened with Mr. Montgomery, yesterday. I know I made the right choice, but part of me keeps wondering if maybe...

No. I shake my head, trying to push the thought away, and I glance at the shameless boy in front of me. "I taste—"

"What she tastes like is none of your business."

I turn around so fast I almost trip on my own feet. Ben is here *again*. He's standing a few feet from me, his heavy coat and wool scarf still on.

"You need to stop" I tell him, an anxious undertone to my steady voice. "Seriously, what the fuck?"

A glint of flaming anger burns in his eyes, but it's gone in a second, replaced by a cautious look. "Please. I know I fucked up last night—"

"That's an understatement" I interrupt him. "And I don't care if you were drunk, upset, or possessed by the devil himself. You don't get to act like that."

He runs his hands through his brown hair. "I know, okay? I made a mistake and I hate myself for that. I despise myself." He spreads his long arms. "Isn't that enough?"

Enough? Oh, God, is he serious?

"I don't know what you expect from me" I mumble, heading toward table six. The lady sitting there keeps waving at me. "I don't want to be with you, Ben."

He's immediately at my heels. "Just because you're stubborn. You refuse to see that—"

"To see what?" I hiss. "That you're a controlling, toxic jerk? That you're unable to accept a no? Trust me, I see that just fine."

He grabs my arm, yanking me toward him, and I stop thinking: I catch a half-full cup from the nearest table and drench Ben in lukewarm tea. For a second he doesn't react: he simply stares at me, eyes wide, tea dripping from his pale face.

"Don't you dare grabbing me like that again" I growl, taking my arm back. "Don't you dare, Ben!"

"What's going on here?"

Fuck. Fuck, fuck, fuck, fuck, *fuck*.

Not him, not now.

I keep my eyes closed, hoping Joseph's words are directed at someone else, but it's unlikely: the café is silent, and I can hear his footsteps coming closer.

"Coral, what the hell?" he says, and this time there's no doubt he's talking to me. "Are you out of your mind?"

I slowly open my eyes. Joseph is standing in front of me, his eyes glancing at Ben. He's trying to dry off his face with his scarf.

"He won't leave me alone" I defend myself. "What else was I supposed to do?"

"I have no idea, but it's not my problem anymore." His stare is cold, when he looks at me, but I can make out the hint of a smile hiding under the surface. "You're fired."

Fired. *Fired.* No, absolutely not: I cannot afford to lose this job.

"No, hey, Joseph." I follow him, not entirely aware of the people watching me, following my every move. "Please. You can't just fire me."

He doesn't even turn to look at me: he simply strides across the café toward the back, where his office is. "I just did."

"I was trying to protect myself, you know?" I insist on the verge of tears. "Please. I need this job."

He reaches for the office door and turns to me for a quick glower. "Not my problem anymore. Take your stuff and get out of here."

I'm tempted to say something else, like a really bad word, but I keep quiet. It would be useless: Joseph decided to fire me months ago. He was just waiting for an excuse to do so, and I gave him a perfect one.

"I hope you're happy now" I say loudly, turning to face Ben. "Was this your plan? You thought getting me fired would make me reconsider the situation?" I force out a laugh. "You're delusional."

"Coral, come on, you know that—"

"All I know is that you need to get fucking lost" I roar, power walking toward the staff-only area. "Don't come near me again or I'll call the police."

And I will, if he does something else, but at the moment I have something more important to think about: what am I going to do now?

CHAPTER SEVEN

The doorbell rings at exactly nine pm.

Even though I know who's behind the door, I still look through the peephole: I don't want any more surprises today. When I recognize Piper's big curls, I open up.

"What's going on?" she asks, coming forward for a hug. "Are you okay?"

Behind her, Sasha holds up a plastic bag. "We have wine and butter cookies. If you're not okay, you'll be soon enough."

"Come on in" I murmur, stepping away. I lock the door as soon as they're both inside. "I'm sorry I've asked you to come here last minute, but…" A sob forces me to stop mid-sentence. "God, I'm sorry. I truly am."

"Hey, hey, stop" Piper says, her voice gentle. She drops her coat on the couch and closes the distance between us in a few strides, her cold fingers brushing away my tears. "It's going to be okay. Tell us everything, alright?"

I do: I describe what happened at the café, careful not to leave out a single detail, as I help myself to more wine than I should.

"Those fucking scumbags" Sasha rumbles, fingers tight on her plastic cup. "Both of them. I can't believe your boss fired you instead of calling the cops on Ben."

"But you will, right?" Piper says, her eyes big and watery.

"Call the cops."

I hesitate, lowering my head. "I mean… If he does something else, yeah."

Piper grabs my elbow, and her warm, alcohol-filled breath brushes my face. "I'm sorry, but what if it's too late? What if he hurts you?"

"Piper's right" Sasha mumbles, putting her feet on the coffee table. "You know, my blackmailing proposal still stands."

"No illegal solutions. Coral, seriously." Piper gives my elbow a gentle squeeze. "Report him. I don't want you to get hurt, please."

I look at her for a long moment before turning my head the other way. "I will, I promise, but right now I have bigger issues."

"Such as?"

"I don't have a job anymore" I sigh, sinking into the couch. "Blood money will only cover so much and…"

I stop talking, silence filling the room.

The money I make selling blood isn't enough to survive, but what about the offer I turned down just yesterday? That kind of payment would be more than enough to live and pay off my current debts.

"Coral?"

"She's probably thinking about illegal solutions" murmurs Sasha. "I approve. There's no other way to get rid of that creep."

I straighten my back, my gaze bouncing between the two of them. "I may have something."

Piper frowns. "We're not talking about illegal stuff, are we?"

"A job" I explain. "Well, a source of income, actually. A gloomy and intimidating vampire wants to drink my blood for ten thousand dollars a month."

Sasha spits out what looks like a gallon of wine. "Excuse me, *what?*"

42

"Yeah." Piper nods, not acknowledging the drops of wine dotting her right arm. "What?"

"It happened yesterday. I turned it down because… because…" I shrug, my thoughts foggy. Again, why did I turn it down? Why is it a bad idea to do it? I already sell my blood for a much lower price. This can't be that different, right? A bite won't kill me.

"You know what, I think I'll give him a call" I mutter, getting off the couch. "He was willing to go higher. Only a stupid would say no to an offer like this."

"Coral, no" Piper protests, but she can't even stand up: she's too drunk. "Do you know him? Who's this person?"

"He's a vampire, not a person" I correct her, as I grab my purse from the floor. "And he's just a rando who found me through that new blood clinic. I told you about that, right?"

"Precisely. It could be dangerous."

"Do it" Sasha says, pouring herself another glass of wine. "It's worth the danger. And if you don't, I will."

Piper tells her something and they start bickering, but I don't listen: from the dark depths of my bag, I've just retrieved Mr. Montgomery's business card, the one I found in my jacket pocket shortly after our encounter. He probably let it slide in when he was so close without me noticing. I debated throwing it away, but I couldn't bring myself to do it—a stroke of luck, right now.

I grab my phone, enter his number, and start the call, charging it to him. If he's really interested, he'll accept it.

The phone rings and rings. I pace around the room, my heart beating faster by the second, and then my eyes land on the wall clock: it's well past one a.m. He'll probably…

"Yes?" A low, groggy voice fills my ear. "Who is it?"

Crap. I've woken him up. I consider hanging up and pretending it never happened, but then he talks again.

"Speak now or I'll make sure you regret this pathetic excuse of a prank."

"Not a prank" I stutter, my tongue heavy and swollen in

43

my mouth. "I, huh… It's me. Coral Deveraux. We talked at the blood clinic, uhm… yesterday, even though it's more like two days ago, since it's past midnight."

There's silence for so long I start thinking he hung up on me, but then I hear a deep sigh. "So, you *do* realize it's extremely late for a weekday."

"Well, I mean… I guess so. But I couldn't wait any longer."

"Is that so?" His voice is serious, but I can tell he's smiling. That, or I'm more intoxicated than I thought.

"Hm-hm" I confirm, still pacing in the semi-darkness of my one-bedroom apartment. "You see, I thought about your offer. Only a stupid would turn it down, and I don't like to think of myself as a stupid."

"And yet I recall your firm rejection, Miss Deveraux."

"Am I not allowed to change my mind?"

"You most certainly are" he replies, his voice deeper than ever. "I'd like to know the reason."

I'm too drunk to stop and wonder whether being honest would make me look rude: I just tell him the truth. "I need the money. Badly."

There's a long pause, then I hear him clicking his tongue. "I see."

"Well?" I push, when I realize he's not going to say anything else. "Is your offer still valid?"

"I'm not discussing the matter right now, Miss Deveraux" he answers, his voice flat. "You're clearly intoxicated and not in your right mind."

"I'm more than able to—"

"I'm not discussing the matter right now." His tone is firm, steady. He's not changing his mind, I fear. "We can schedule an appointment tomorrow. I'll have a car come pick you up at nine a.m."

I shake my head, even though he can't see me. "To go where?"

Again, there's a long pause. "My office."

44

"You know, I have my own car" I state, my words coming out a bit distorted. "I can drive, Mr. Montgomery."

"Nine a.m. sharp. Be ready."

And with that, he hangs up the phone.

Well, just great.

CHAPTER EIGHT

Drinking so much was a mistake.

My head is pounding, I'm nauseous, and my face looks like it belongs to a corpse. I'm also very much late: the car Mr. Montgomery sent to pick me up has been waiting for the past fifteen minutes.

Well, it's not my fault: I told him I could drive, and he ignored me, so that's on him.

I run out of the bathroom, limping on one foot to put on the left boot, and I grab my purse from the coffee table. I stop there for a second. Piper and Sasha are sleeping on my couch, all tangled up and peacefully snoring. I consider waking them up to let them know I'm leaving, but ultimately, I decide against it: drunk Piper wasn't a fan of my plan, sober Piper would lock me in to prevent me from going.

And I get it: it's not the most brilliant plan I could come up with, but I have no other choice. I give my friends one last look, then I'm out of my apartment.

The morning is crisp and cold, too much for my thin and worn-out coat, but at least the car is heated.

The driver is very quiet: beside a quick nod while opening the car door for me, he hasn't acknowledged me in any way—he's simply driving along the busy streets of the city, completely focused on the road ahead of us.

The car looks expensive: leather seats, black, matte surfaces, tinted windows. That's no surprise: Mr. Montgomery seems really well off. I mean, in order to offer me ten thousand dollars a month just to feed off me, he must be.

It doesn't take very long to get to his office: after a fifteen-minute drive, the chauffeur stops the car and jumps off to open my door.

We're right in the heart of the city: the street is lined with staggering skyscrapers, so tall they poke the clouded sky; men and women in tailored suits march on the sidewalks; the road is packed with cars and yellow cabs, the crispy morning air filled with chatter, engines roaring, and loud honking.

My driver points at the building in front of us. It's a tall structure made entirely of glass and steel. Above the revolving doors, there's a big, metallic sign: it says Montgomery Industries.

"Ask of Mr. Montgomery at the front desk" the driver says. "Someone will escort you to him. I'll be here to take you back home when you're done, Miss."

I thank him profusely, and then I'm on my own.

By the time I'm at the front desk, telling my name to the male receptionist, I'm questioning my decision. Am I really that desperate? Am I willing to do to this just for some cash? The answer is yes to both questions, so I gladly accept the badge the receptionist is giving me, and I follow him past the turnstiles in the lobby.

"So…" I start, as we're waiting for one of the elevators to get down here. There's three. "Mr. Montgomery. He works here, right?"

Stupid question, I know: the building has his name on it. But I had no idea how to start the conversation.

"Founder and CEO" the receptionist confirms, giving me a side glance. "I thought you knew. You're not here for a job interview?"

I hesitate. Technically I sort of am, so I nod. "Yeah. It was all last minute, so I didn't have time to catch up with all the… info. You know."

The central elevator saves me: the doors open with a loud ring, letting out a man talking in a shiny earpiece.

Apparently, Mr. Montgomery's office is on the 80th floor. *Eightieth*. And it takes less than a minute to get up there. The area is big, airy, and bright, with glass walls and fake plants in the corners. We walk past spacious cubicles, most of them empty, and we stop in front of a big, closed door. Not that it matters: it's transparent, made of glass, just like the walls surrounding it. I can clearly see Mr. Montgomery sitting at his desk, busy typing something on a matte laptop.

The receptionist knocks, and he doesn't even lift his gaze: he simply makes a quick gesture with his hand, like anything else would be too much of an effort.

"Miss Deveraux for you, Mr. Montgomery" the receptionist says, pushing the door open. "Need anything else from me, Sir?"

"No, Miles. You can go."

He retreats, and for a moment, I wish he wouldn't: last night I felt bold and confident, but right now I'm far from that. I'm afraid I'm missing some liquid courage.

"You're late."

That's his warm, comforting greeting. Not that I was expecting anything different from him.

"Well, you didn't tell me at what time we would be meeting" I argue. "You said you'd send a car to pick me up at nine a.m."

He slowly lifts his head to look at me. His gaze is dark and impossible to read. He's not amused, that's for sure. "Precisely. It takes fourteen minutes to drive from your apartment to my office, Miss Deveraux." He points at the minimalistic wall clock on his right. "It's now nine thirty-one, making you fifteen minutes late."

"You haven't considered traffic."

"The traffic conditions were ideal, this morning." He leans forward, his gaze not leaving mine. "I made sure to check."

Yeah, right, of course. I haven't been here two minutes and he's already pissing me off. "Okay, I was late. Sue me."

"You will find out I do value my time, Miss Deveraux."

"Then why are we wasting it?" I reach the desk in two strides and sit down on the glass chair directly in front of him. "Let's go over your proposal. I value my time as well."

For a second, he does nothing besides staring at me. His gaze is so heavy I'm forced to lower my head, a weak attempt to stay calm and collected.

At last, he sighs. "I had a contract drafted by my attorney." He takes a stack of papers from a drawer and slides it toward me. "Read it."

I'm about to say that a thank you or a please wouldn't kill him, but I keep it to myself—he's too intimidating.

The contract is short and simple: ten thousand dollars at the beginning of every month, deposited directly in my bank account, in exchange for my blood. It's a year-long contract, a span of time in which I pledge to take good care of my health, sell my blood solely to him, and be available whenever he needs me.

There's a particular line that almost makes me laugh: *The quantity of required blood may vary, but the contractor commits himself to never drink more than the recommended amount, in order to guarantee the donor a safe experience.*

"Something funny?"

I give him a quick look, realizing far too late my lips are curved in a smile. "Sorry, it just feels surreal."

"I sure hope you're not about to change your mind again, Miss Deveraux."

I hold his stare for a few seconds, then I look back at the contract. "Here it says that when you call, I must comply immediately."

"Is that a problem for you?"

"Well, I go to college" I explain to him. "It's not like I can leave in the middle of class just because you want a snack."

Am I hallucinating or is that a *smile*?

"A snack" he repeats, as if he found the word amusing. "I believe we'll be able to work something out each time, depending on the circumstances. Something else?"

"As a matter of fact, yes." I lower my eyes on the contract again, scanning the text to find the next point I want to bring up. "Here it is. Why does it say that while this contract is still effective, I won't be able to sell or donate my blood elsewhere?"

"Because I'll take everything I can, Miss Deveraux." Mr. Montgomery's voice is deep, his gaze dark and intense. "Anything more would result in health complications we surely want to avoid."

I find myself unable to answer. He's not wrong, and for ten thousand dollars a month, I can afford to make him my only buyer.

"And what if I want out before the end of the year?"

"Haven't you read the fine print?" He arches an eyebrow. "Right at the end. Go ahead."

I do as he says, quickly scanning the last page of the contract, and soon I find out what he's talking about. "A penalty fee of one hundred thousand dollars?" I look at him, my eyes growing bigger and bigger. "Are you kidding me?"

"A matter of self-preservation. A warranty, if you will."

"What if I get sick and I'm forced to terminate our contract?"

He keeps his eyes on me, his face an emotionless mask. "Then we will reevaluate accordingly."

I'm still not entirely sure I want to go ahead with this, but what choice do I have? I count to ten, then I grab a pen sitting on the desk and sign every page of the contract—both copies. It's done. There's no turning back now.

Mr. Montgomery signs the contract as well and hands my copy back, his fingers already typing on the shiny surface of his phone. "You should have received your first payment. Mind to verify?"

What? Already?

I grab my phone from the front pocket of my bag and log into my bank account.

"Holy crap" I whisper, unable to contain myself.

Ten thousand and six dollars—those six dollars were all I had left before the transfer. It feels unbelievable.

Mr. Montgomery gets up and walks around the desk, his steps slow and deliberate. "I suppose the payment went through smoothly."

"Yeah" I murmur, forcing myself to close the app and lock the phone. "Thanks."

"No need to thank me. I'll make sure to fully benefit from my investment." He arches his eyebrows. "Now get up."

Crap. For some reason, I bypassed the thought he would drink from me *today*. I mean, why wouldn't he? The contract is signed, and he's already sent me the money. It makes perfect sense.

When I get up, my legs are shaking, and my stomach is tied up in knots; I can feel my hands grow clammy with each passing second.

Mr. Montgomery doesn't look like a bloodthirsty creature. Everything about him suggests control: his dark, pushed-back hair, his cold gaze, the smoothness of his pale skin, the way his jaw contracts, his perfect posture, the grey shirt tensing over his broad shoulders, the bulging veins on his exposed forearms... I can't imagine him with blood dripping from his mouth and that look of dreamy bliss in his eyes— the one all vampires have after drinking. I actually don't even know if that's the truth: I've only seen it on television.

"Miss Deveraux." His voice falls flat, but there's an annoyed edge to it. "May I proceed?"

I'm shaking, but I force myself to nod and expose the left side of my neck. "Suit yourself."

God, please, don't let me die. I have so many things I need to achieve.

Mr. Montgomery moves forward. His movements are slow—he's not in a hurry: it looks like he's taking his time to do this, enjoying every second of it.

He places a hand on my back, while the other is busy brushing my long, raven black hair away from my neck. He leans in, one painful inch at a time, and his warm lips touch the skin of my throat.

Then he bites me.

His sharp teeth sink into my flesh, right in the curve where the neck meets the shoulder, and the blood starts flowing.

God. It's really happening.

Aside from the first sting, when his fangs pierced my skin, it isn't really painful: all I can feel is a tingly sensation as Mr. Montgomery's warm mouth sucks my blood.

How is this so nice? Am I out of my mind?

His grip on me grows tighter, to the point my chest is pressed against his and I'm forced to arch my back.

I don't mind. His body is strong and radiates heat—with his mouth sucking and licking and kissing my sensitive skin, I'm almost tempted to completely abandon myself in his arms.

"I almost went insane, Miss Deveraux" he murmurs, his lips still on me. "All because of you."

I can't answer, I don't want to: I'm too busy enjoying the tip of his tongue brushing over my wounds, the fresh scent of his aftershave, his strong hands holding onto me like he's afraid I'll run away.

He finishes too quickly: he backs off, handing me a tissue for my bleeding wound, and I have to stop myself from looking disappointed. I have no idea why, but I want him to drink some more: that feeling is so strong, so overpowering... It's what I imagine an orgasm would feel like. Too bad I've never had one to actually make a truthful comparison.

Mr. Montgomery licks his bloody lips; my lower belly, at the sight, twitches. "Excellent transaction."

"Yeah" I stutter. "Very... nice."

"You need assistance to head back down?" He's not smiling, but there's definitely a different glint in his eyes. An ironic, mischievous glint. "I can find someone to escort you."

I hold his gaze even though I can feel my cheeks getting warmer. "I'm perfectly fine, thank you."

"I'm glad."

"So, huh…" I nod toward the office door. I was so lost in the moment I didn't even consider anyone could see us through the glass walls. Great. "I better get going. You know, college and stuff."

He stares at me with such intensity I feel like I could burst into flames at any given moment. "Keep your phone near, Miss Deveraux." His lips form what's almost a smile. "I have a feeling we'll be meeting again… soon."

CHAPTER NINE

"It's a mistake, Coral. What were you thinking?"

I need to hold back a groan. I regret telling everything to Piper: I know she's only trying to look after me, but most of the time, she overdoes it.

"I need the money" I remind her, squeezing my phone tighter. "It's not like I enjoy it…"

That's a lie. A big, huge lie, but I really can't tell Piper I enjoyed letting Mr. Montgomery suck my blood: she'd have me locked up in a mental institution in no time.

"You could always find something else" she insists. "You know how I feel about vampires… Yeah, they're mostly integrated, but some of them are still out of control. Have you heard what's happening in Russia?"

"Just like some humans." I push the broken door open and walk into the dark, humid hall of my apartment building. "And no, I haven't heard, but I have a feeling you're about to fill me in."

"They took control of most of the country" she explains. "They overthrew the government, Coral. Do you realize how dangerous this is?"

Dragging myself up the stairs, I hold back a deep sigh. "Okay, you're right, some of them are nuts. But Mr. Montgomery… well, he's chill. A bit stiff, but chill, nonetheless.

He didn't hurt me, did he?"

Piper doesn't answer immediately. I almost hear her brain working full force to produce a convincing argumentation. "Doesn't mean he won't do it in the future."

I deeply inhale, but I don't get to defend my point: I climb up the last step of the staircase and stop dead in my tracks, my eyes growing wide.

Ben's here: he's sitting in front of my apartment, knees bent, thumb mindlessly scrolling on his phone.

"Fuck" I whisper, still as a statue.

He still hasn't seen me: I could silently head back down and seek shelter in the nearest café, waiting for him to go away.

"What?" Piper says in my ear. "You okay?"

Too late. Ben looks up from his phone and his gaze lights up. "Coral, hi."

"Oh, my God, don't tell me it's that scumbag. I take back what I said: the vampire is a thousand times better."

"Call you back in five minutes, Piper" I mumble, my eyes following Ben's every movement. "Love you."

She tries to say something, but I immediately hang up: I can't afford to get distracted.

He gets up from the floor and wipes the dust from his pants. "Where were you? You didn't have any classes today."

I actually had two classes—this means he doesn't know my schedule for the new semester. That's a relief.

"It's none of your business" I answer, making sure he's not getting too close. "What are you doing here?"

"Baby, don't be like that."

"Don't call me baby, Ben."

He stops, his lips so tight they form a straight line. "I get it, you're mad. I overstepped the other day."

I shake my head. "That's the understatement of the century."

"But you were the one who threw hot tea on me" he says, his hands lifted as he takes another step forward. It's like he's

58

approaching a wild beast. "You were kind of asking for it."

Asking for it? *Asking for it?* "Have you lost your mind?" I shout, my heart pounding in my chest. "You made me feel like I had to protect myself! How is this asking to get fired?"

"Okay, okay, calm down. I'm not here to argue." He takes another step. "I'm just trying to make amends."

"I'm not changing my mind" I warn him, as I start retreating down the stairs. "So you can stop trying, Ben. You're just wasting your time."

"Could you just… Could you listen to me for a fucking second?" There's a hint of rage in his eyes, but he manages to get it under control in a moment. "I didn't want you to lose your job, okay? But it happened and I'm sorry, Coral, I really am." He takes a deep breath. "I wanted to make things better, so I found something for you. A new job."

I frown. "What are you talking about?"

"Remember Kath, that old friend of mine from high school?" he asks. "She works for that big chain of night clubs… Lust at first bite. I don't know what she does there, but she told me they were looking for someone and I gave her your info."

"What kind of job is it?"

Ben shakes his head. "I don't know. She said they needed someone good looking, so maybe waiting tables? Here." He grabs a piece of paper from his pocket. "Her number. She said she'd give you a call in the next few hours, but if you need to contact her for whatever reason… you can."

I reluctantly take the number. "Okay. I'll think about it."

I don't mention I don't need this job, and not only because I refuse to let Ben know about my latest deal—part of me knows I still should work. I have all my debts to pay out, my daily and monthly expenses, I'd like to move out from this nightmarish apartment… and then there's the little bookstore *maman* and I always dreamed to open. I usually don't let myself indulge too much in the fantasy: I'm well aware I don't have the kind of money for that. But now, with

Mr. Montgomery's generous offer, I can see the outline of a possibility.

I start doing the math in my head, but Ben interrupts me.

"Is that all?" he asks, expectation in his big, blue eyes. "Nothing else?"

I'm tempted to call him an asshole and push him down the stairs, but I'm pretty sure that'd be attempted murder. Not in the mood for jail.

"You've been... considerate" I say, even though finding me a new job is the least he could do. I lost mine because of him. "Thank you."

"Don't I deserve another chance?"

"I don't know if you deserve it." I quickly walk past him, and before he can catch up with me, I run for the door, key ready in my hand. "What I know," I say, unlocking the door and sliding in, "is that I don't want to give it to you. Stop harassing me, Ben."

Just as he's starting to move toward me, I close the door and lock it as fast as I can, bracing myself for his uncontrollable rage.

It never comes, though: after a few seconds of total silence, I can hear light tapping from the other side of the door.

"You and I belong together, Coral" Ben says, his voice quiet and collected. "And soon enough you'll see it as well. I have no doubt about it, baby."

I choke down a scream of frustration.

When will he leave me alone?

CHAPTER TEN

The Lust at first bite is an exclusive nightclub—there's an entire chain of them, actually, all scattered around the US and Europe.

The one I'll hopefully be working in is located in one of the most exclusive neighborhoods of the city, where the elite (and wealthy vampires) like to party. Not the kind of place where I usually hang out: it's out of my price range and I deeply dislike nightclubs. Working in one is fine, though.

At six p.m. Kath welcomes me in her office, a big room in the back of the club. I don't know what her role is here, but it's pretty obvious she'll be the one deciding whether I get this job or not.

"I still don't know what kind of occupation this is" I say, sitting down on the chair in front of her. "Ben… he didn't say it."

Kath looks at me for a long moment, a curious glint in her eyes. "Because he doesn't know. He would've withdrawn, and honestly, I couldn't afford it."

I frown. "What do you mean?"

"We need a new stripper" she explains, a half-smile on her lips. "I don't think he would like the idea."

"Ben and I aren't together anymore" I quietly explain. "So, I honestly couldn't care less about what he doesn't like."

"I see."

There are a few moments of silence, then I look up. "I thought I'd be waiting tables or... I don't know, clean around. I already have experience in that field."

"You also have experience in this field."

"Stripping?" I shake my head. "No. Sorry."

Kath grabs her phone from the desk and angles it toward me. On the screen there's a picture of me during an old performance: I'm standing in the middle of the stage, wearing a black tutu, black pointe shoes and a black mask. I look fierce, even though ballet has always been my least favorite kind of dance—I liked modern dance way better.

"I was a dancer" I tell her. "Not a stripper."

"You're not forced to strip." She locks her phone and puts it back down. "Our girls are mainly dancers. Some of them like to incorporate stripping to their routines or shows, but it's not a requirement."

I hesitate. There's nothing wrong with being a stripper: it's a respectable job like any other. It's just the thought of being at the mercy of so many men with potential malevolent intentions...

"We have a strict no touching policy" Kath says, as if she's read my mind. "Nobody touches you unless you give them explicit permission."

Jesus. Am I really thinking about it?

"What would I need to do?" I ask after a second of hesitation.

Kath proceeds to explain everything: shifts, clothes, work etiquette, money...

"On a good night you could go back home with three thousand dollars" she points out.

"Three... Three thousand dollars?"

Kath smirks. "Not so bad, huh? You'll have to build a solid client base, and that may take some time, but I trust you won't face big problems in this sense."

Crap. That's insane. I quickly do the math in my head:

even with slow nights, I should be able to save a nice amount of money in no time, all doing something I love—dancing.

"When do I need to start?"

Her smile gets bigger. "Is tonight a problem? We're short staffed and could really use some extra help."

Is it a problem? I don't know. Between this and Mr. Montgomery's money, with the right decisions on my part, I could really change my life for the better.

I look up, determination and excitement and anxiety coursing through my veins at the same time. "I'll do it. Where do I need to sign?"

After showing me the club, giving me the combination of my locker, and encouraging me to buy clothes and shoes from the shop in the back, Kath leaves me alone in the changing rooms.

Tonight, I'll be working from eight to midnight. It's simple: I get out there, on the big platform (specifically in Area number four), and I dance for whoever is watching, then I collect the tips.

"First day?"

I look up. The girl sitting at the vanity next to mine, a redhead with plump, shiny lips and huge fake lashes, is smiling at me.

"Hi. Actually, yeah." I scratch my neck. "Is it so obvious?"

"No, it's just we all know each other, and you're a new face." She extends a tan, lean hand. "Jasmin. Nice to meet you."

"Coral."

"Well, welcome on board, Coral!" she exclaims, looking back at the mirror. "Are you on a trial period?"

I nod. "Two weeks. What about you? How long have you been working here?"

"About a year." She starts sectioning her hair with a comb. "Before this I was dancing in a hellhole of a tavern where the average client had a criminal record three feet long. Talk about improvement!"

Jasmin is very nice: she openly talks about her experience at Lust at first bite, how she's treated, the money she's able to make on an average night, the reason she's working here— pay for her studies.

"I want to become a biologist" she says. "What about you? What brings you here?"

"Oh, I…" I shrug. "Debts, mostly. And I'm saving to open a bookstore, in the future."

For the first time ever, that elusive idea appears a tad bit more tangible, to the point I don't feel like a fool saying it out loud.

I don't know how this thing will turn out, but I'll try my best. Of this, I'm sure.

CHAPTER ELEVEN

A loud banging startles me awake.

I jump up, crumpled blankets tying my legs together, a bitter taste in my mouth.

What time is it? What's this noise?

I look around, my vision blurred and my thoughts confused. Buttery beams pour in from the window, painting random spots of light on the floor.

Another two bangs echo throughout the apartment. It takes me a second to realize it's someone knocking at the door.

Not Ben again, please.

I can't deal with him, not right now—I'm too tired. It's been three days since I've started working at the Lust at first bite, and with finals season approaching, I haven't been sleeping at all. I can't complain, though: the job is good. Clients have started to request me for private dances, and they all pay well. Yeah, I get the occasional nasty comment about *what else that body can do*, and there's been a few creepy dudes making *proposals*, but it isn't hard to ignore them.

Today's the first day I don't have any classes, and I wanted to take this opportunity to catch up on some rest.

No: I'm not dealing with Ben today. It's not fair.

He knocks again, and even though I can't really tell, he seems a bit more impatient.

"Go away, Ben" I shout toward the door. "I'm trying to get some sleep and I'm not opening the door."

"It's Lev Montgomery, Miss Deveraux."

Oh, crap. Mr. Montgomery. What is he doing here? What does he want? His first name is Lev?

I jump down the pull-out couch, instinctively fixing my knotted, sweaty hair, and smoothing the oversized t-shirt I use as pajama.

I'm a mess. Not my fault, though: he's the one who showed up here unannounced. I have every right to look ugly and disheveled in my own apartment, especially this early in the morning.

"Are you planning on leaving me here all day?" he says, his voice slightly annoyed. "I have places to be."

Then go, I'd like to say, but I keep it to myself: I don't want to cause unnecessary tension.

I put on the first pair of sweatpants I can get my hands on and drag myself toward the door.

He looks extremely out of place standing in the hall outside my apartment: his tailored suit, shiny black hair and perfect posture clash with the peeling wall and the smell of piss coming from the staircase.

He's hot, hot enough to make my heart throb and my insides twist.

"You do realize it's practically the middle of the night?" I ask, scowling at him—a stupid attempt to hide how happy having him here makes me. Happy, excited, a bit nervous. The feeling of his mouth sucking my blood is still fresh in my mind, still makes my skin tingle.

He arches an eyebrow. "It's eight in the morning, Miss Deveraux."

"I went to bed at four."

"Why is that?"

I cross my arms. "I believe that's none of your concern. Why are you here?"

He keeps quiet for a long moment, eyes scanning my figure

in search of answers I'm not going to give him. "I've been trying to contact you. Your phone number is unavailable."

"Oh, yeah…" I scratch my neck. "My phone died last night, and I forgot to plug it in. I was too tired."

"I thought I'd made myself clear." His stare is icy. "I want you to answer when I call."

"My bad, sorry" I say, suppressing a yawn. "Come on in. I'd offer you a coffee or something, but I feel like you're here to drink something else."

As he comes in, eyes studying my messy and very small one-bedroom apartment, he fights back a smile. "Intuitive. Miss Deveraux, you live *here*?"

"Intuitive" I mock him, closing the door. I point at the cluttered table in the corner. "Please, sit. I just need five minutes to…" I nod toward the bead curtain separating the bathroom from the rest of the apartment. "Make yourself at home."

Before he can say anything, I grab some clean clothes and get in the bathroom. Luckily the shower sits behind the wall, meaning he won't be able to see me.

God. He's about to bite me again, and I honestly shouldn't be this excited. What's gotten into me?

I take the quickest shower ever and wear the clothes I've taken with me—mom jeans and a cropped sweater—then I brush my teeth. I come out of the bathroom barefoot and with my hair still wet.

Mr. Montgomery—Lev—hasn't sat down: hands pressed in his pockets, he's scanning the books filling my small bookshelf. He even looks interested.

"I told you to make yourself comfy."

He turns, his expression unreadable. "I'm in a rush. You're making me late, Miss Deveraux."

"How rude." I frown. "I took a cold shower so I'd be clean for you. Don't tell me you'd like to bite into sweaty skin."

Mr. Montgomery moves forward, a ghost of a smirk on his full lips. "Sweat doesn't concern me."

"Then next time I won't make an effort to smell good,

since you don't appreciate it."

In the span of half a second he materializes in front of me, crowding my space. It's not the first time I see him do this trick, but it disorients me, nonetheless.

I try to back off, but his arm wraps around my waist, holding me against him. God, he's so warm.

"You always smell good" he says, his voice low and raspy. He leans in, his nose caressing the skin on my throat. "You smell heavenly, Miss Deveraux."

I try to suppress a gasp with little success. "I think you can start calling me Coral" I whisper, unable to find my voice. "We're a bit past formality, aren't we?"

"As you wish" he murmurs. "Right now, you could ask for an entire constellation, and I'd buy it for you."

"A few books will do."

He grabs a fistful of my wet hair with his free hand, forcing me to tilt my head back.

I should be scared: I'm in a vulnerable position, my bare throat at his mercy, his strong hands caging me—and yet, all I feel is expectation.

I take in his warm lips tracing an imaginary line on my skin, his firm grip on me, the minty smell of his aftershave…

When he finally bites me, I let out something that awfully sounds like a whimper. I couldn't care less: the only thing on my mind is the overpowering sensation that makes my body tremble and shiver. I can't get enough of this feeling—my blood flooding his hot, greedy mouth, his teeth scraping my flushed skin, our bodies so tightly pressed together. It's addicting.

"You're intoxicating" he groans.

His lips are still on me, but to my dismay, he's not sucking anymore. I can tell he's fighting some sort of internal battle: he's stiff, his breathing ragged, his arms prey to a slight tremor. It's like he can't bring himself to get away from me. I don't want him to: I feel like I'll fall down without his strong arms holding me, and not because he's drunk too much blood—it's something else entirely.

Before I can say something, he steps away and tilts his head back, smacking his blood-stained lips.

Why is this so hot? Why am I tempted to lick his mouth clean and…

I shake my head and walk to the table, where I grab a scrap of paper to stop the bleeding. It feels like my legs are going to fail me at any moment.

"From now on, I expect timeliness on your part." Lev's voice comes from behind me, so close I can practically feel his warm breath on me. "Don't make me repeat myself, Coral."

Or what? Part of me is curious—eager to know. His deep voice is full of promises… or maybe I should say threats, the kind I might happen to like.

"Otherwise, there will be consequences."

My stomach is in knots as I turn around to face him. His mouth is clean, but there are still traces of blood in the cracks of his lips. He's looking at me with such intensity I can barely make eye contact.

"What kind of consequences?" I ask, my heart pounding so fast he can probably tell.

He tilts his head, a curious glint in his dark gaze. "I'm not sure you want to find out."

I bite my lower lip and wisely choose to say nothing, but his words affect me a lot. Unusual images flood my mind: tangled up bodies, exploring hands, exposed skin… a lot of exposed skin.

I never make this kind of thoughts. I don't get these urges; I deeply dislike sex—assuming what I did with Ben was sex. We were never able to make it past foreplay, so I'm not entirely sure.

We were together for a long time, but with him, I never felt this way.

What's going on?

CHAPTER TWELVE

One of the men below the stage waves a stack of bills. "Take off that bra and these are all yours!"

The lights are low and there's smoke all around, but I can tell it's a lot of money. Not enough, though: I'm not undressing—not on stage and neither during a private dance, no matter how much he has to offer.

I ignore him, focusing on the slow rocking of my hips. The song blasting through the speakers is slow and sexy, my favorite kind: at least I don't have to go wild on these goddamn heels.

"Talking to you, number four!" he insists, still waving his money. "I know you can hear me!"

I don't acknowledge him: I keep on dancing, giving my attention to the small crowd on the right. I get on my knees, knowing damn well how hard it will be to get back up, and I slowly slide down. I roll on my back, almost squirming on the stage, my hands caressing my overheated body. I can't help but imagine Lev doing it: judging by the way he grips me when he drinks from me, I suspect he'd know how to make me feel good. Really good.

As soon as the song ends, I get up and collect the tips from the crowd, just like Jasmin taught me. It's a nice sum. I'm about to thank them for their generosity, when my eyes lock with those of a man in the back of the room. I don't have trouble recognizing him: that dark gaze is unmistakable.

What the fuck? Did I just manifest him?

Lev doesn't have the dissolute expression I gave him in my fantasy: he's angry. Fuming, actually. He starts making his way through the crowd, but before he can get close enough, someone calls me from backstage. It's Anita, the dancers' assistant.

"You've been booked for a private dance" she says. "VIP room two. Be quick, Coral, the client made it clear he doesn't want to waste any time."

It's the fourth time I get booked for a private dance, and it's honestly one of the things I dislike the most about this job: being alone in a room with someone who's lusting after me, dancing only for them in an allusive way... It makes me uncomfortable. Thing is, I don't want to turn the requests down: they pay very well.

I get off the stage and stop by at the changing rooms to freshen up a bit: I retouch my makeup, smooth out my French braids and fix my outfit—a black lacey set with fishnets and sparkly heels.

The VIP rooms are in a secluded area of the club, where only members can get in: casual clients aren't allowed inside. I enter VIP room two from the backdoor, and I immediately notice I'm not alone: the client who's requested me is already here. I also happen to know him: it's the man who was trying to convince me to undress.

"Hello, number four" he says, smiling at me from the chair he's sprawled on. "What's your name?"

I wish I could tell him I like 'number four' just fine, that he can keep calling me that, because he gives me the creeps, and I don't like the idea of sharing any kind of information with this man—not even my stage name.

"You can call me CC" I answer, mimicking his smile. "Thank you for booking me, sir. I hope you enjoy the show."

He licks his lips in a way that makes me want to throw up.

"I have a feeling I will, CC."

I twirl around, taking a bit too much time to turn on the music system, then a force myself to put on a seductive face as I walk toward him. It feels like venturing in the direction of a rabid beast, eager to devour me.

No touching policy, I tell myself, and I hope he remembers as well.

I start swaying with my arms up in the air, letting the music guide me through this.

"Come closer" he murmurs, his eyes following my every move. "Just a little, yeah?"

God, I so don't want to. I force myself to take a step forward, and the moment I do, he leans toward me and grabs my wrist.

"No touching" I remind him, but when I try to back off, he doesn't let go. "Sir, it's against the rules. Let me go."

He shakes his head, a mischievous grin on his lips. "I don't appreciate being ignored."

"I don't get undressed, end of story." I try to get rid of him and pull my arm free, but he's too strong. "Let me go."

"You disrespected me" he hisses, his smile hardening into a grimace. "I don't let anyone disrespect me, especially whores like you."

I don't see it coming and neither does he: a big hand closes around his forearm, squeezing it.

It's Lev. I didn't even realize he was here.

"What the fuck?" the man exclaims, his head jolting up. "Let me go!"

Lev's gaze is unreadable, but his stiff posture tells me he's angry. "I'll revaluate your request when you let *her* go."

On the other hand, the man is clearly upset: his face is getting redder and redder, his body is shaking. "Who the fuck are you?"

A mean, cold smile appears on Lev's lips. "The owner of this place."

The owner? Is he for real?

The man hesitates for two seconds, then his grip loosens: I can take my arm back. It's sore, and there's a red mark where his hand has been.

"Don't let me see you here again" Lev says, his voice dangerously low and calm. "Do I make myself clear?"

The man mumbles something under his breath, looks at me for a fraction of a second, then quickly retreats toward the door. He's gone.

There's a long moment of silence before I gather the courage to utter a shaky 'thank you'.

At first, Lev doesn't react: he keeps his eyes on the door, almost expecting to see the man barge back in, his shoulders stiff with tension.

"Thank you" I repeat. "He wouldn't let go."

He slowly turns, a hard expression on his sharp face. "Care to explain what on earth you are doing here?"

I shrug. "Work?"

"As a stripper, it appears. Why?"

"Dancer" I correct him. "I don't strip. Even so, what's the big deal?"

Rage flashes in his eyes, but he's able to keep it under control. "This is no place for you."

"I'll be the judge of that, if you don't mind" I reply, irritation building inside me.

Why is he so angry? Is it because I'm invading his working environment? Well, it's not like I did it on purpose: I had an opportunity, and I took it, simple as that.

"I needed a job, and I found this one. It pays well."

"*I* pay you well" he points out. "Isn't ten thousand dollars a month enough for you?"

I don't shy away from his gaze. "It's none of your concern, Lev."

For a second, he looks lost, uncertain of what to say.

"What?" I cross my arms, arching an eyebrow. "I'm not allowed to call you by your first name?"

"It's not that. I…" He shakes his head, that unusual hesitation already lost. "It doesn't matter. I don't want you here, end of story."

"But why?" I exclaim. "I had no idea you were the boss here. It's not like I choose this place on purpose just to annoy you!"

His expression hardens. "You think that's the reason I'm mad? Because you annoy me?"

"I mean, why else would you react this way?"

At first, he keeps quiet, his eyes lingering on my exposed body. His gaze is so intense I feel shivers running down my spine. Then he sighs, slowly shaking his head. "You don't annoy me, Coral. But this is no place for you."

"I'm an adult" I reply. "Why wouldn't it be?"

He gets in front of me so fast I don't even have time to process his movement. In the span of half a second, his hands are on my hips, dragging me closer. "Because this is a place of perdition. Of self-destruction. A place where dreams come to die." His gaze scans my face, lingering on my lips for the longest second of my life. "I don't want you to end up like that."

I don't know what to say. That's unexpectedly thoughtful, but his snooping around in my business still doesn't sit right with me. "What do you know?" I ask, my voice unsteady. "Maybe I like working here. Maybe I enjoy doing this job."

"Oh, yeah?" he murmurs, his voice raspy and low. There's an angry glint in his eyes. "Show me. Dance for me, Coral. Right here, right now." He grabs his wallet from his tailored pants pocket and takes out a stack of bills, waving it at me. "Make it sexy. I'll be sure to compensate you accordingly." A cold smile spreads across his lips. "Is three hundred dollars enough for a lap dance? I can go higher, but some of those clothes need to come off."

His words wound me like sharp knives. Why is he treating me this way?

"What the hell is your problem?" I snap, pushing him away. "I won't let you treat me like this. *So* not happening."

"See?" he snaps back. "You're not a good fit for this place. You can't deal with this shit!"

"You know nothing about me!"

"I know you enough to realize you shouldn't be here!"

"Go to hell, Lev Montgomery!" I shout, but before I can walk away, he grabs me by the waist and pulls me toward him. He's so close I can feel his heat: it makes my skin prickle and quiver with anticipation.

"Only if you come with me" he mutters, and in a second his mouth is on mine. I can taste blood as he parts my lips, his kiss greedy, imposing and overwhelming—just like him. He's frantic, impatient, as if he couldn't get enough of me, his hands exploring my skin under the top.

Fucking hell.

This definitely isn't my first kiss, but none of those that came earlier can compare to this one. My knees wobble, my stomach is in knots, and I'm about to beg him to rip my clothes off.

I step back as soon as I realize what's happening, my feet unsteady on these horrible heels. I touch my lips, still tingly from our kiss, I give Lev a quick look.

"I need to go" I mumble, retreating one step at a time. "I, huh… I…"

I can't even finish my sentence: I glance at him one last time, then I run off.

CHAPTER THIRTEEN

I'll simply forget everything and move on.

I decide it the next morning, after a long, sleepless night spent dwelling on whatever happened between me and Lev. No, Mr. Montgomery, *just* Mr. Montgomery: getting so close to him was a mistake in the first place, one I intend to rectify immediately.

I don't do relationships anymore, not after Ben: one obsessive ex-boyfriend is more than enough to deal with.

After getting ready for the day, I grab my purse and leave my apartment, making sure to lock the door behind me. For once I'm not late—given I haven't slept one minute, I consider this a huge victory.

I make my way down the stairs, adjusting the scarf around my neck, but as soon as I step outside the apartment building, I stop dead in my tracks.

It's Lev—I mean, Mr. Montgomery. He's standing in front of a shiny, black car, one of those elegant and slender models I always see in movies, never in real life. Fair enough: Mr. Montgomery himself is the kind of man (pardon, I meant vampire) I only ever see in movies. He's wearing a grey button up shirt and black trousers, a suit jacket resting on his right shoulder.

"Coral." He steps toward me, a cautious look in his eyes.

"I've been calling you."

Yeah, I know: I ignored his calls because I was mad and confused and... other things, things I'm not ready to admit even to myself.

"I don't want to talk to you right now" I say, but when I try to walk past him, he moves to stand in my way. "I'm late to class. Please let me go, Mr. Montgomery."

He shakes his head. "Last night you called me Lev. Keep doing so."

"I've come to the conclusion it's inappropriate" I reply, trying to keep my voice steady. "We're just two parties involved in a transaction. Let's not forget that."

"Coral."

"Miss Deveraux, if you don't mind" I correct him. I'm trying hard to keep my cool, but my heart is pounding so fast I feel like he can hear it. "Let's keep our distance."

He gives me a vicious smile as he leans in, his fresh scent filling the air. "Keep our distance, huh? Because yesterday you didn't seem to think so."

"*You* kissed me!" I hiss, taking a step back.

The smugness in his expression doesn't change one bit. "You let me kiss you. You enjoyed it, Coral."

"Miss Deveraux. And... And..." I stutter, taking another step away from him. "None of this matters. It's inappropriate. All about last night was."

"Fine" he murmurs, coming forward with a dark glint in his gaze. "Let's keep this appropriate, shall we? Bare your throat, *Miss Deveraux*. I still haven't had breakfast."

God. He's talking to me as if I were just a walking blood dispenser. I guess that's exactly how he sees me, given his attitude.

"You can't talk to me like that" I reply, my voice cracking. "It's rude. Treating people with human decency is free and accessible to everyone, Mr. Montgomery, even you."

He takes another step forward, his eyes growing darker and darker. "Bare your throat. I won't repeat myself another time."

"Or what?" I ask, forcing out a nervous laugh. "Will you take what you want by brute force?"

"You signed a contract. I expect you to fulfill your half of the deal."

I can't believe him. What's his problem? Why is he acting this way? I'm so angry my hands shake, and I don't see clearly anymore. How could I be so stupid? How could I ever involve myself with this absolute prick?

"You know what?" I snap, unable to stop myself. "Fuck the contract. I'll give you your damn one hundred thousand dollars, but I want out. Immediately!"

Anger flashes in his eyes, the only sign he's actually furious: his body is still perfectly still and controlled. "Don't be ridiculous. I know you don't have that kind of money."

"The job at the club pays well" I tell him, raising my voice. "And if it's not enough, I'll just become a hooker. Now if you'll excuse me, I have places I need to be."

He calls me back, but I ignore him. I may have put myself in a difficult situation, but I know myself: I'll be able to find something. I have to.

It's a slow night at the club, probably because it's only the middle of the week. I've made a total of nine hundred dollars, though, so I won't complain.

Only about ninety-nine thousand left to repay Lev… I mean, Mr. Montgomery. Not so bad.

I'm about to step out of the changing rooms, eager to head home and take a long shower, when someone calls my name from behind my back.

"Coral?"

I turn around. It's Kath, walking toward me with a tense expression. I don't see her often: she usually spends her time taking care of business in her office.

"Everything okay?" I ask, as she stops in front of me.

"Not really. There's a… situation."

Crap. Last time I heard this sentence, it was because a cocky vampire had corrupted who knows how many people to find me. It's not exactly a great omen, given how that turned out.

"What kind of situation?" I frown. "Am I in trouble?"

Kath quickly shakes her head. "No, absolutely not. I…" She hesitates, her eyes scanning me with a glimpse of interest. "How do you know Lev?"

"Lev Montgomery?"

"The boss, yeah."

It's my turn to hesitate. I know many people get involved in this type of deals, but there's still a stigma surrounding the whole idea—especially among mortals. I know Kath won't judge (she works in a club popular among vampires, after all) but there's no point in telling her: I already called it quits. I still have to decide whether to congratulate myself or shoot my own foot for it.

"We met randomly some time ago" I tell her. "Why do you want to know?"

She takes her time before answering my question. "He's at the bar counter, drunk as hell… asking about you. *Demanding* to see you." She bites her lower lip. "He's pretty upset. Did something happen?"

I hold my breath. If he's drunk, it means he took something strong: normal alcohol doesn't affect vampires.

"I don't know" I mumble, crossing my arms. "Maybe. What do you want me to do?"

"Get him to leave. He's scaring clients away."

"He won't listen to me" I scoff.

Kath arches her eyebrows. "He asked for you. Repeatedly. He won't let anyone else come near him."

Then let him rot there, I think, but I don't say it out loud. I'd never admit it, but I'm a bit worried. Is this about the fight we've had this morning? Is he that upset?

He deserves it.

Yeah, that's probably true. Still, when Kath heads toward the end of the hallway, telling me he's in the main room of the club, I follow. I'll make sure he gets home safely and then I'll leave myself. Easy peasy.

We walk into the room. The lights are bluish and purple, sluggishly pulsating, and a slow song flows from the speakers of the music system. We make our way through half-empty tables and stop by the counter, occupied by one person only—I mean, one vampire only: Lev. He's sitting on a stool, hunched over a multitude of empty glasses.

Kath nods in encouragement, pointing at him.

"Mr. Montgomery?" I mutter, taking a step forward. "What's going on?"

He slowly turns his head to look at me. "I told you to call me Lev" he mumbles, his words melting together. "I like it when you call me Lev."

"Alright, Lev" I say, getting closer. "Time to go home, okay?"

He drinks from his glass. I can't see what's inside, since the glass is black, but the sip leaves his lips bloody. "You're coming with me."

Not a question, rather a command. What a prick.

"I'll make sure you get home safely" I clarify. "Then I'll go back home as well. *My* home."

A mix of emotions cross his face: anger, discomfort, affection, longing, anger again. Turns out he's not always in total control of himself: good to know.

"I don't want you to work here."

"Yeah, you made that pretty clear" I say, helping him down the stool. "But you don't get to decide for me, Lev. I'm a big girl."

He leans in closer, holding onto me to balance himself. He's so close, I can feel his warmth, his breath caressing my overheated face—it stinks of blood and something else.

Kath steps in, handing me a set of keys. "His car is outside. I sent his address to you. If you need anything, just let me know."

"I sure hope you're going to pay overtime, Kath."

She smiles, waving at me. "Bye and thank you!"

"I know you're a big girl" Lev murmurs, apparently unaware of my playful banter with Kath. His darkening eyes are set on me like nothing else currently exists. "I still hate the idea of you working here."

"Come on" I joke, guiding him across the room. "Just say you're jealous."

He stops dead in his tracks, forcing me to stop as well to avoid a bad fall. In the pulsing lights of the club, his eyes look like black holes—tempting ones, that's for sure.

"I *am* jealous" he says, not a hint of hesitation in his voice. "Didn't you know?"

I'm speechless, opening and closing my mouth without actually uttering a word. "I was… That was a joke" I stutter, painfully aware of his arm resting on my shoulders. "I didn't mean that."

He holds my gaze. "I did."

God, he's obviously rambling, fueled by whatever he got drunk with, and yet… and yet my stomach feels all knotted, and my legs start to shake.

No, I promised myself: no more relationships. Ben was enough.

"You're drunk" I whisper, gently pushing Lev toward the exit door. "You don't know what you're talking about." I give him a quick glance, then turn my head. "Let's just get you home."

CHAPTER FOURTEEN

Of course, Lev lives in a penthouse in the city center, one of those places you only see in interior design magazines and Netflix shows.

I've struggled to drag him from the underground parking lot to the elevator, his dead weight all over me, but it's worth it: this place is incredible.

The elevator's doors open directly into his living room: the area is huge, with minimal, black and white furniture, and an entire wall made out of glass—the city's skyline is a map of shining lights, an ocean of fireflies glinting in the dark.

I limp on the glossy marble floor, dragging Lev across the room. We walk past a set of sleek, leather armchairs and a TV area that could compete with a movie theatre, but then I have to stop: there are a few doors on the far right, an open kitchen on the left, and a spiral staircase right in the middle of the living room: I don't know where to go. There's no way I'm dragging his heavy ass all around this uselessly large apartment.

"Where's your bedroom?" I ask, trying to shake Lev awake.

He cracks his eyes open, a sly smile curving his mouth. "What for?"

"Dump you on your bed" I answer drily. "You're heavy."

"Just wait till I'm on top of you, then" he replies, his voice deep and raspy, an amused edge to it.

"You won't. Bedroom, *now.*"

He looks at me for a never-ending moment before pointing at one of the doors. "I like how impatient you are."

I ignore him, even though his delirious flirting is leaving a mark. A deep one, too. Why do I enjoy his attention? Why is it so nice to hear him say these things?

I don't indulge my inappropriate thoughts: I secure my grip on Lev and drag him to the door he pointed at, pushing it open with my right hip.

Wow. Just wow.

The king-sized bed is in the middle of the room, covered in gray silky sheets, only two pillows on it. It lays on a thick rug, and it's sided by two empty nightstands. On the left there's a big sliding door (probably leading to a walk-in closet), on the right floor-to-ceiling windows overlooking the city.

I can't believe there are people waking up to this view. It's crazy.

"I know you like what you see" he mumbles, as I shove him toward the bed. "It could be yours, Coral. All yours. Including me."

"Oh my God, just shut up and go to bed." I push him down, but at the last moment he grabs the collar of my shirt, so I fall on top of him. "Lev! What the fuck?"

"You want to leave me." There's a whiny and accusatory edge to his voice.

I try to get back up, but he won't let me: for a wasted vampire, his grip on me is strong. "Yeah, because you're a bossy prick. I hate bossy people. Now let me go."

He ignores my request, holding me even tighter. "I've been an asshole."

"Definitely, yeah. Can you let go now?"

"But I can't stand the idea of you dancing for other people" he continues, as if I hadn't spoken. "Of them fantasizing about you."

I try to push myself up and away from him, but it's pointless: it's like I'm glued to his warm, heaving chest. "This sounds like a you problem."

"I want you for me, Coral."

I hold his gaze until I can't anymore, then I look down at the first undone buttons of his shirt. "It's the alcohol talking" I reply, trying to keep my voice steady. "Now let go, Lev. I need to retrieve my car at the club and head home."

"It's the truth" he murmurs, pulling me even closer. "I'm not that drunk."

"That's exactly what a super drunk person would say."

One of his hands slides up and grabs my ponytail, gently forcing me to look up. "I know you feel it too."

His gaze is gloomy, intense, heavy, but this time I can't look away: I'm attracted to it like a moth to the light. I know it'll hurt, but I can't really help myself.

"I don't know what you want from me" I whisper, unable to talk louder. "I don't get it, Lev."

He doesn't answer immediately. His fingers trace imaginary lines on my back, circles, weird figures I can't quite make out. Then he closes his eyes and pulls his hands away. "I don't know either."

I shouldn't feel disappointed, and yet here I am, wishing he hadn't said what he just said, wishing he hadn't stopped touching me. I hesitate for a moment, then I push myself up, trying to ignore how my body is rubbing against his. I need distance. Lots of it.

"I have to go now" I mumble, smoothing down my messy hair. "Try to sleep. It's going to be better in the morning."

He doesn't move: he simply keeps staring at me from the bed, stretched out on crumpled sheets, his eyes carrying unsaid truths I'm both scared and curious about.

"It won't if I wake up alone" he says, his voice deep as a crash of thunder. "Stay. Please."

That *please* is far more unexpected than the fact he wants

me to stay. Is he capable of politeness?

"I won't let you feed off of me in this state" I reply, painfully aware of my shaky voice. "There's no guarantee you'd be able to control yourself. I don't have a death wish."

A sharp, cruel smile tugs at his lips. "So naive. I could drain you dry in less than a minute, if I wanted to. Intoxicated or not."

"That's not reassuring, you know?"

"My point is," he says, an amused edge to his voice, "yes, I could. I haven't, though, nor do I have any intentions of doing so." His gaze follows my every move, captured, making my skin tingle. "That's not why I'm asking you to stay. I just want you close for a while."

I shouldn't even give him an answer: I should turn around and walk out of this apartment without looking back, because the situation is starting to get dangerous—and not because he's a bloodthirsty vampire.

I don't move a muscle, though. I stand very still, very quiet, my eyes caressing his relaxed body. I want this. I want to be close to him, even though I don't have any rational explanation for it. I just like how having him near makes me feel, how my body reacts to his, how well we fit together.

"I hope you're not expecting to have sex with me, because it's not happening" I impulsively say, as I feel my cheeks getting warmer.

He cocks an eyebrow. "Do you believe I'm trying to fuck you? How weak do you think my seduction game is?"

"No sex" I insist, taking an uncertain step forward. "No matter how convincing you are."

"Trust me, Coral" he mutters, a mischievous glint lighting up his eyes. "When the time comes, it won't take any convincing." His grin is devilish. "You'll be ripping your clothes off."

"I... What?"

He answers with a smile that makes my insides twist with anticipation. And then he closes his eyes, his breath becomes calmer, his body relaxes even more. I didn't think it was possible to fall asleep so fast, but here he is, proving me wrong.

I hesitate. I shouldn't stay, right? It doesn't matter how good I feel when I'm next to him, it doesn't matter how much I want it—I shouldn't.

I don't go, though. The mere thought is frustrating. I want to feel his warmth on my body, I want his hands on me, his lips on mine, his teeth sunk in my flesh.

I don't have the strength to get away from him. Maybe I'll try again tomorrow, but right now, I can't.

So, I hop on the bed and lie down next to him, knowing damn well I'm going to regret it.

CHAPTER FIFTEEN

When I open my eyes, the bedroom is flooded with morning light, beams so bright they threaten to blind me.

I blink, but when I try to sit up, I find out that I can't: a strong arm is wrapped around my waist, pinning me down on the mattress. I follow the bulging veins on the forearm, the creases on the rolled-up sleeve of the shirt, the defined biceps stretching the fabric... Still asleep, Lev is something nice to look at: his messy black hair brushes his forehead and closed eyes, as he breathes with his plump lips slightly parted. He looks pretty, not as sharp-edged as he usually does.

I should've gone away last night. Now it's morning, who knows how late, and leaving will be twice as hard—let alone dealing with my complicated emotions and whatever happened only a few hours ago.

He won't remember, I tell myself, trying to gather the courage to face the day. *And I can still leave before he wakes up, right?*

I don't even have my car. I'll need to go back to the club, retrieve it, and drive directly to class, because there's no way I'll be able to stop at home to shower and change.

My very first walk of shame... and I didn't even have sex. Just great.

Lev's arm is holding me tight, but I manage to slip away from his grip and hop down the bed. I try to be very quiet as I fix my clothes and put my boots back on, controlling my every movement and breath, but it's pointless: in the span of one minute, Lev's eyes flutter open and land directly on me.

"What are you doing?"

Good God. His morning voice puts his normal voice to shame: it's deep and raspy and gruff, the words pronounced *oh* so slowly.

"Last night you—"

"I know" he cuts me off, rubbing an eye. "I remember."

Well, there goes my plan to turn a blind eye on what happened. I was hoping the hangover would make him forget.

"Where are you going?" he asks, sitting up on the crumpled sheets. "That's what I meant."

"I have class and my car is still at the club." I finally get a hold of my purse, forgotten on the dresser, and I pull my phone out. It's seven thirty. "I'm running late, so I better get going."

"Would you grant me one minute before you go?"

I stop by the door, my back to him. "Why?"

There's a moment of silence before he says anything. "To properly apologize. You deserve it, Coral."

"Yeah, I do" I mutter, crossing my arms. "You acted like a douchebag."

Behind me, I hear fabric rustling and slow steps coming closer. "I did. And I'm sorry about it."

No buts? No excuses?

I can feel him stop behind me, too close and at the same time not nearly enough. "You still spent the night" he softly murmurs. "Why?"

I'm not going to confess that's exactly what I wanted, because I'm not ready to admit it to myself, let alone him.

"Well, you were in a terrible state" I reply, trying to control my shaking voice. "It didn't feel right to just… leave you here alone. I'm a decent person, you know?"

With the tip of a finger, he traces a line up my back. When he reaches the end of my loose ponytail, probably messy and frizzy, he moves it on my right shoulder so that he can keep drawing his imaginary stroke along my spine. His touch is light, and yet, it's all I can focus on right now.

"You're much more than a decent person, Coral" he says in a husky voice. He's so close I can feel his words, made of warm breaths and untold promises, intertwining with my hair. "And I don't want to lose you. Reconsider your decision."

I gather all my courage, up to the last splinter, and I turn around. He towers over me, his hair messy, his eyes pools of liquid darkness. There's something in his expression I can't quite place: it's not rage, it's not bloodthirst... it's a primordial feeling, one that runs deep and almost makes him vibrate with an energy I'm drawn to.

It's desire. Pure, powerful desire.

"Always so bossy" I mumble, trying to recollect my emotions and thoughts, which are currently all over the place. "I don't like bossy people. I already told you."

"*Please* reconsider your decision" he asks again, and the way he says it makes it seem like he's actually struggling to be polite. "This deal is beneficial for the both of us."

"Will you stop commenting on my job?"

His jaw stiffens, and a few seconds pass before he speaks again. "Can I ask why you're working there?"

"I have debts to pay off" I explain, happy with the small progress we're making. "My bills are through the roof, my textbooks cost me a fortune, and... and I'd like to open a bookstore, someday." I give him a quick look. "Our deal isn't permanent. I need to be prepared, Lev."

He's quiet for a few seconds, considering, evaluating what I've just told him. Then he cocks his head, staring at me. "Twenty thousand."

"Twenty thousand what?"

"I'll give you twenty thousand dollars a month if you quit that job" he explains, unfazed. "Is that an acceptable amount to take care of your situation?"

I blink, then I shake my head. "It's not about the absurd amount of money you're willing to pay. I need something stable."

"Being a stripper at the club is anything but stable" he replies, his cold voice stained with anger.

"Dancer" I remind him, taking a step forward. "I don't strip. Also, it pays well, and it doesn't interfere with my class schedule." I cross my arms. "It's not my dream job, but for now I can settle."

Lev shakes his head. He's trying to hide his emotions, but the mask on his face is cracking and I'm starting to recognize what's beneath. I don't like it. I don't like it one bit.

"You shouldn't have to" he says, as he pinches a loose strand of my hair. "You should never have to settle."

"It's just how life works." I lower my gaze as I take a step back. "And since you're obviously not going to stop bothering me about my job, it's better to call it quits." I take a deep breath. "I'll find a way to give you what I owe you. Now if you'll excuse—"

He grabs my elbow, his grip firm but gentle. I could easily shake him off and walk away, but I don't. It's like I was secretly hoping he would stop me.

"I don't want your money, Coral" he says, so close I feel his breath touching my face. "I will refrain from commenting on your job, you have my word. But I beg you, reconsider."

I open my mouth, close it, open it again. I can't make a sound, let alone a coherent sentence. "I think... No, I know you'll find someone else. Someone with tastier blood than mine."

"No blood can compare." He pulls me closer, and I let him, even though I know I shouldn't. "No person or vampire can compare."

"Lev…"

"You're the one" he says, and then he sniffs my bare throat. "My mate. You always have been, from the very first moment."

I take a step back, my heart pounding in my chest. I know vampires have mates, individuals with whom they spend all eternity, but it's always other vampires, definitely not humans. I can't be his mate. I just have a kind of blood he happens to thirst after.

"I'm not a vampire" I breathe, taking another step away from him. "You're mistaken, I'm not you mate. I'm sorry."

He shakes his head. He looks calm and collected, but the crack on his mask keeps getting bigger and bigger. I can tell he's frustrated. "It does not matter. You are my fated mate, Coral."

"I'm nobody's mate" I whisper, shaking my head. "And nobody's mine. I don't... I'm not..." I make a big gesture with my hands. "I don't do relationships, not anymore."

Lev moves toward me. In his dark gaze flickers a glint of light. "I know you feel it as well."

"I don't know what you're talking about."

I know exactly what he's talking about, but there's no way I'll admit it. This whole situation is getting too big for me to manage. I just want out.

"You do" he replies softly, as he closes the distance between us. He grabs my hips and suddenly my heaving chest is pressed against his, so solid and warm. I instinctively arch my back, my hands rising to meet his shoulders, and at the same time he leans in. "You do. It's that sinking feeling in your stomach, that craving to keep me close, those shivers on your skin." He places a small kiss behind my ear, but doesn't move away: when he talks again, he does it with his lips touching my neck. "That orgasmic feeling you get when I bite you... I get it too. All of it."

He does? So I'm not going insane?

"I, huh..." I'm struggling to focus—he's too near, his lips on me hot. "I don't know what you're expecting from me."

His lips don't leave my neck as he asks his next question. "What do you mean?"

"I told you I don't do relationships" I breathe, resisting

the urge to close my eyes and simply give in. "And sex is a big no for me. So, you telling me about this mate thing…"

"I don't expect anything from you" he murmurs. "I'm just asking you to please reconsider your decision."

I take a deep breath, my fingers sinking in his shoulders. "Only if we can keep this professional."

The tip of his tongue licks that soft spot under my jaw. "Define professional."

"No unnecessary touching" I reply, fighting to hold back a moan. "No kissing. No talking about this mate thing."

"What about this?" His grip on my waist tightens, to the point he almost lifts me off the ground, and he slides his tongue up my throat. "Is this considered professional?"

I have to suppress a whimper. "Most definitely not."

"That's such a shame" he mutters, before placing a kiss on my jaw. "Such a shame."

"Please… Lev." I swallow, forcing myself to focus on what's going on. "Drink if you need to, but… stop. Stop this. I can't take it anymore."

"So our contract is still valid?"

It almost feels like he's doing it on purpose to convince me, but I'm not mad. I'm confused and overheated and something else, but not mad. Despite my words, I'd let him do anything to me, right now.

"It is" I reply. "Just… let's just stick to the rules and we're good. I'm sure we can do it."

But the moment the words leave my mouth, I know for a fact they're not true.

We won't be able to do it.

CHAPTER SIXTEEN

"Sorry, guys, I can't. I'm busy tonight."

"Doing what?" Piper asks, her voice crackling from the other end of the phone.

"Doing *who*?" is Sasha's contribution, a muffled voice I barely recognize. "Is it that sexy vampire who's paying to drink your blood?"

I feel my cheeks grow warmer, and I'm glad this is not a videocall, because I know for a fact I'm blushing. Nothing would scream 'guilty' like that.

"No" I sigh, playing with my car keys on my lap. "We don't… it's not that." I glance at the backdoor to the club, barely visible in the semidarkness of the parking lot. The streetlamps placed along the road behind me don't help at all. "I have to work."

I can almost feel Piper's judgmental stare on me. "At the club he owns?"

"It's not like it was intentional" I mumble, unbuckling my seatbelt. "And it's not like he's planning my murder, P. Can you relax a bit? It's fine."

"Not really" she replies, a hint of resentment in her voice. "It's the third time in a row you cancel on us."

I open my mouth, and then slowly close it again when I realize she's right. A few days ago, we were supposed to meet and work on a group project for our Ethics class. I had to re-schedule because I was too exhausted from working the night shift, and then yesterday I had to reschedule again because I was so tired after spending the night at Lev's, and now…

I can't believe I've acted this way with my only friends, the ones always willing to help and support me. What kind of person am I?

"I'm so sorry" I say, shaking my head. "I'm a… I've been a shitty friend, haven't I?"

"Amen to that" Sasha's muffled voice replies. "We still love you though."

Piper's sigh is loud and clear. "It's not that you've been shitty, Coral. We know you have a lot going on. We're worried."

"Yeah, no, she's been shitty. Canceling for three times in a row is definitely shitty behavior, if you ask me."

I bite my tongue, pushing back the tears collecting at the corner of my eyes. "Sasha's right. I fucked up and I'm so sorry, guys. It's been…" I shake my head, grabbing my purse from the passenger seat and hopping down the car. The air is freezing, and my breath comes out in big foggy clouds. "I don't want to make cheap excuses. You deserve more than that. What about tomorrow? We can get lunch together and then work on our project, if you're both available."

"Lunch is on you?" Sasha's muffled voice asks.

I nod, even though she can't see me. "Lunch is on me. What do you say?"

"You don't have to" Piper intervenes. "But it's a good idea, nonetheless. Where do we want to meet up? At what time?"

We figure out the specifics as I enter the building and make my way to the changing rooms, and by the time I've pushed my stuff inside the locker, we're all settled.

"Sorry again, guys" I mumble, biting the inside of my cheeks. "I promise I'll do better."

"Just don't blow us off again and we're good. See you to-morrow!"

"See you tomorrow. Love you!"

106

Just before I can change into tonight's outfit—a glittery silver leotard with a deep neckline and shiny high heels—Kath bursts through the door, eyes scanning the room. When they lock on mine, a faint smile appears on her lips. "Good, you're already here."

"Everything alright?" I ask, a cautious edge to my voice. Last time she was looking for me, Lev was dead drunk at the bar counter—and all that happened next is something I won't forget that easily.

Kath nods, stopping next to my locker. "You've been booked for your entire shift. VIP room one." She glances at her wristwatch, a small smile tugging at her lips. "You better hurry. He seemed eager to have you all for himself."

"He?" I question her, playing with the belt of my robe. "Who is he?"

Her grin grows a tad. "You'll see. I'm glad everything worked out between you too."

I don't know why, but my first thought is that the man waiting for me is the one who wanted me to undress, the one Lev made run away with no effort. Could it be him? Has he found a way to come back?

As I get dressed, I tell myself it doesn't matter—I'm safe here. If it's actually him, I'll be able to refuse him the service. I'm not forced to do anything.

I do my makeup base, then I put on some shimmery eyeshadow, a thin layer of eyeliner and fake lashes, finishing the look with a generous coat of lip gloss.

I'm ready.

That knot forming in the pit of my stomach highly disagrees, but I ignore the uncomfortable feeling and head to the VIP rooms, reminding myself it's going to be okay.

"Totally okay" I breathe, stopping in front of the door to VIP room one. "And if it's not, I get to walk away. Easy peasy."

I take one last breath, then I push the door open, walking inside. The room is bathed in purple and pink neon lights, strangely soothing, and a song is already playing from the stereo system.

It takes me one second to spot the only other person standing in the room, and when I realize who it is, I have to hold back a snort. How comes the most obvious answer escaped me so easily? Of course, it's Lev. I'm not even surprised to find him here.

"You said you wouldn't interfere with my job" I say, stopping by the door. "What is this?"

He turns, his movements slow and controlled; when he's facing me, all stiff and serious looking, his eyes scan my figure with the softest touch. And then they darken, a heavy shadow settling on his gaze. It takes me a long moment before I realize it's not rage—it's desire.

"You're three minutes late" he states. His voice sounds firm, but his words carry a degree of wickedness I can't quite ignore. It makes me quiver.

"You're not supposed to be here" I argue, crossing my arms. "It was part of the deal, Lev. You're making me regret it."

For a few seconds, he stays quiet. He takes his time to look at me, his stare so intense I can feel myself starting to blush. I can't help but wonder how I look like in his eyes. What is he seeing? Does he like it? And I know, I know it shouldn't matter one bit, but it does—I can't help it.

"I'm not interfering" he says at last, his voice deep and raspy. "I'm paying good money to have you here."

"And do what? A sexy dance? A little striptease? Because I'm not comf—"

He interrupts me with a flick of the wrist. He's pointing at the table and chairs placed at the center of the room. "Actually, I was hoping to watch you study."

"Study?" I repeat, rapidly blinking. "Huh?"

"Study" he confirms, taking a step forward. "You know… books, highlighters, notes. I'm sure you know what I'm talking about."

My gaze lands on the table, where a neat stack of books is

set beside a pink case and a laptop. *My* laptop and *my* pink case. The books are mine as well.

"What is going on?" I ask, turning my head to face Lev. "Why is my stuff here?"

He holds my stare with ease, his chin slightly tilted upwards. "I thought I'd made myself clear. I'd like to watch you study."

"You've booked me for the entire night to watch me study?" I shake my head in disbelief. "How did you even manage to get that stuff?"

"You left it at my place." A sly grin stretches his lips. "You were in such a hurry to flee you forgot your school bag."

I hadn't even realized I had it with me, that night. Now that I think about it, I haven't seen my college stuff in a few days. I guess I was just too tired to care.

"I'm... that's not..."

As I'm tripping on my words, he circles me with lazy steps, only stopping when he's standing right behind my back. "I'm paying well" he mutters, his breath warm against my exposed neck. "I promise."

I need a few seconds to collect myself, mission I accomplish with the help of some deep breaths. "Why are you doing this?"

"I could have you fired, but I'd never stoop so low." With the tip of his finger, Lev traces the seam on the back of my leotard. "I believe this is a fair compromise."

I turn around, but I'm not ready to face the look in his eyes: it's burning with feelings I'm all too familiar with. I lower my head, forcing myself to breathe. "If you get jealous of me dancing half naked for other men, it's not my problem." I gather my courage to quickly glance at him. "I'm not yours, Lev."

"I'm trying to fix that" he murmurs, his eyes lingering on my figure.

Not without a hint of horror settling deep in my stomach, I realize I want him to. I want him to make me his, I want to be around him, find out all the little things he likes and despises, I want him to make me whimper his name.

"I already told you" I mumble, unable to voice my sudden realization. "I don't do relationships. It's not my strong suit."

He takes a step toward me, his fingers caressing my chin, gently pushing it up so that we're looking at each other in the eye. "And why is that?"

I press my lips together. I debate telling him—about my relationship with Ben, how it made me scared of being intimate with a partner, how I don't think I'm lovable enough.

I don't, though. This stuff is far too personal for me to share. I want to keep this professional, and to do so, I have to respect certain boundaries. This is one of them.

I shake my head, pressing my lips in a tight line. "It would be unprofessional to tell you" I mutter, taking a step back. "You promised, Lev."

He looks conflicted, but at last, he nods with a sharp breath. "Alright, I won't push you." He crosses his arms, the fabric of his button up shirt growing tighter on his torso. "Are you planning on denying me the service?"

I open my mouth and then close it again, my eyes settling on the nicely arranged table. I *do* need to study. And I would be lying if said this isn't one of the nicest gestures anyone has ever done for me—he's been really thoughtful. And a bit controlling, let's face it.

"I don't... You realize you can't always have it your way, right?"

He gives me a smirk. "I can try."

"You're frustrating" I mumble. I'm acting bothered, but in reality, I'm not. Far from it. "You know that?"

"You're the first person to tell me" he replies, his lips still bent in that stomach-knotting half smile. "If you want to deny me the service, I'll accept it."

For a second, I simply look at him. I stare at his sharp features, his pushed-back hair, his perfect posture, his suit that fits like a glove. He's stunning.

"It's not fair" I say, shaking my head. "You're paying me for what, exactly?"

"I didn't picture you as someone with such faulty comprehension skills" he murmurs, leaning in to caress my jawline with the tip of his index finger. "I want to watch you study, Coral. That's what I'm paying good money for."

I take in the feeling of his fingertip on my skin, enjoying it a bit too much, then I take in a deep breath. "It's not one of the services I offer."

"That's why I'm paying double."

"But why? Other than the fact you want to prevent me from dancing for others."

Lev closes the distance between us, tilting his head to whisper something in my ear. "Nothing turns me on more than intelligence." He touches my neck with a brush of his lips, then retracts with a wolfish grin. "Show me what that brain can do."

He actually ends up watching me study the whole night. He sits on the other side of the table, silent, observing, almost raptured by all my muttering and scribbling and highlighting.

His gaze is intense, yet not distracting—I almost find it comforting, an encouragement to keep going.

I'm able to catch up with all my work, turn in a few essays, and even head start with the project I need to work on with Piper and Sasha tomorrow. When I close the last book, it's well past midnight and I'm exhausted.

"All done?" Lev asks, his voice low and vibrating like a purr.

I give him a small nod, busying myself with the mess I created on the table. "That was nice of you, even though your motives weren't entirely selfless."

"I've never said they were." He fishes his phone from his pocket and fumbles with it for a minute, then he nods toward me. "Check if the payment went through."

"My phone is in my locker" I breathe, wetting my lips. "I'll check as soon as I retrieve it."

"Is your shift over?"

"Yes. Do you..." I point at my throat. "You know. Do you need to drink?"

He shakes his head. "Not tonight" he says, and then he flashes one of those smiles that leave a burning mark deep in my stomach. "Is that disappointment I'm reading in your eyes?"

"I... no. Of course not." I clear my voice and take a deep breath. "I was just... you know, I thought... Doesn't matter."

"Tomorrow" he states after a while. "I'll see you tomorrow, if that's alright with you."

"If that's alright with you" I repeat, an incredulous edge to my voice. "Who are you? Where's Lev Montgomery?"

He leans forward, over the table separating us, and stares at me with such longing I feel my skin burn. "He's trying not to be such a bossy prick."

"Good... Good for him" I stutter, unable to hold his gaze for more than two consecutive seconds. "I mean, good for you."

"Do you need a ride home?"

"I, huh..." I point at somewhere behind my back. "I have my car, but thank you."

He cocks his head, an eyebrow slowly rising to brush against a dark lock of hair. "I've seen your car. It belongs with a museum."

"What?" I launch myself over the table to smack him on the arm. "Take that back *now.*"

"Take back the truth?" He raises his eyebrows, but it's clear he's fighting a smile. "I have my morals, you know."

"My car is vintage and perfectly working, thank you very much."

"When was the last time you had it checked?" he asks, inclining toward me. "I bet dinosaurs were still around."

I make a scene by opening my mouth and resting my left hand on my chest, but I'm genuinely impressed: I didn't think he was able to joke. "You're using *sarcasm*? What's going on?"

"There are sides of me you don't know, Coral. I'm more than a bossy douchebag."

"Shocker, honestly."

"Let me drive you home" he murmurs, leaning even closer. "Let me replace that fossil with something safer."

"Lev… no. Highly unprofessional." I look at him with a determination I didn't know I had. "You're not my boyfriend. Even if you were, it wouldn't be your job to pay for my stuff."

He tilts his head to the side. "What if I want to?"

"We agreed to keep it professional."

Lev stares at me, unspeaking, his gaze so intense I feel it prickle at my skin. "As you wish."

I nod with a small sigh. "Thank you. So…" I stand up, holding my backpack tight. "Uhm, I suppose we're all done here."

"You've never answered me."

"To what?"

He stands up as well, circling the table to get closer to me. "Can we meet tomorrow?"

"Uhm…" I hesitate for a second, then I shake my head. "I have class in the morning. Also, I'm having lunch with my friends and then we're working on a school project together. I can't."

"Tomorrow night? At your place?"

"I, huh…" I lick my lips. "Yeah, okay. Eight p.m.? Nine? I don't know how long the project will take."

"Let's settle for eight." Lev stops in front of me and pushes a strand of hair behind my right ear. "If you need more time, just let me know."

"Will do. See you tomorrow, then?"

"See you tomorrow."

CHAPTER SEVENTEEN

I need to remind myself this won't be a date. The only reason Lev is coming over tonight is that he wants to drink my blood, and as we agreed, we're going to keep it professional.
I have to keep it in mind.

"Yeah, no, it's definitely a date."

My eyes dart up, meeting Sasha's amused gaze. She's playing with a paper straw, repeatedly knotting it in the middle and creating a giant knot, which is devouring the straw itself.

"It's not. I told you" I mumble, focusing on the melting ice in my drink. "We decided to keep it professional."

"Professional my ass" Sasha laughs, throwing her creation at me. "If you guys are actually mates, there's no way in hell you'll be able to keep your hands off each other for much longer."

I'm starting to regret telling them the whole story, but I had to: I needed their opinions on the situation, I wanted them to reassure me I was doing the right thing, that Lev and I would be able to keep our word… My expectations were clearly wrong.

"You really had to put yourself into this situation, didn't you?" Piper's stare on me is a mixture of irritation and worry. "You're so stubborn."

"Enough with the me talk" I say, before sipping my drink.

"P, your birthday's coming up. Are you planning to do something? Our traditional karaoke night?"

"Oh, uhm." Piper clears her throat and exchanges the quickest glace with Sasha, who's busy torturing another straw. "We haven't told you. Right."

"Tell me what?"

"We're, huh…" She hesitates, wetting her chapped lips with the tip of her tongue. "It wasn't…"

"We're having a mini trip to New York to celebrate" Sasha interrupts her. "A gift from her mom."

"Oh! That's… That's great, guys." I smile, slowly realizing why Piper was so hesitant to tell me. We usually spend all of our birthdays together, doing karaoke, watching cheesy movies, getting drunk, doing each other's nails. This is news. "I bet you're going to have the best time there."

"I'm so sorry, Coral" Piper says, grabbing my hand, her eyes wide. "We're not trying to exclude you or anything. My mom had only enough money to pay for two plane tickets and a double hotel room."

"Guys, no! Seriously, it's fine. I wasn't expecting to tag along! You're dating and it's perfectly normal to do this kind of things together."

I laugh it off, but in reality, I'm a bit hurt. We've known each other for almost five years now, and we usually do everything together, but them dating has changed a lot of things. I mean, I'm happy for them and I know it's just how it works, but I miss how it used to be.

I guess I have my big share of responsibility for this slow yet inexorable shift: I've been growing distant, busy with Ben, work, my constantly empty pockets—I can't blame them for how things are turning out. Sometimes I just wish I could go back in time, act differently.

"We can… If it's fine with you, we can always celebrate when you come back." I shrug with a small smile on my lips. "I know I've been a bad friend, but I'd like to make it up to you. I really don't want to lose you guys."

They exchange a long look, then Sasha bursts out laughing, bending forward. "Oh my god, you should see your face!"

"My f... My face?" I stutter, giving Piper a quick glance. She's hitting Sasha on the shoulder, barely keeping it together herself. "Why are you laughing?"

"It was a prank" Piper explains, then she finally lets herself go, howling with laughter. "Of course my mom booked everything for the three of us, she loves you!"

"What?" I blink, unable to process her words. "I don't... I don't get it."

"We were pranking you because you deserved it a little" Sasha says, still laughing her ass off. "But do you really think we would exclude you like this?"

I hesitate, forcing back a smile. "I didn't know, okay? You two are dating, so it would make sense!"

"Nothing makes sense if we're not all together" Piper says, reaching out to take my hands. "Sasha is my girlfriend, but you're my best friend, Coral. I want to celebrate my twenty-third with the both of you."

"Your face was honestly priceless" Sasha snickers, rubbing her eyes. "You were hurt but trying so hard to hide it... God, I should've recorded it!"

"Yeah, I didn't want to act like a bitch!" I laugh, throwing a crumpled napkin at her. "Of course I was trying to hide it!"

They got me. Who would've thought these two could pull off such a prank? They're better actresses than I thought.

"You guys have no idea how grateful I am to have you" I mumble, my gaze jumping from Sasha to Piper. "You're the two most important people in my life. Come here!" Careful not to knock down the glasses and empty plates littering the table, I lean over and pull both of my friends into a messy hug, Piper's big curls tickling my face, Sasha's bony shoulder digging in my right arm. "I honestly don't know what I'd do without you!"

"Well, at least you acknowledge it" Sasha scoffs, but it's

117

blatant she's holding back another laugh as she hugs me back.

"I love you too" Piper sighs, patting my back. "That's why I want you to rethink about this whole situation with the…" She pulls back to look around, making sure nobody in the pizza place is looking at us. "With the vampire" she hisses, as if it were a bad word.

"Who, the one who's going to fuck her senseless in three days tops?" Sasha wiggles her eyebrows. "Or another one?"

I stare at her, eyes wide, heart beating fast. "Excuse me?"

She simply shrugs. "It's surprising you haven't yet torn the clothes off each other. I've heard mates can't quite control themselves when it comes to—"

"Look how late it is!" I interrupt her, pointing at the big wall clock hanging at the other end of the pizzeria, above the kitchen door. "We should totally start working on our project, or else we won't be able to finish it today. Shall we?"

A lame excuse, I know, but they both drop the subject. Sasha winks; Piper gives me one last glance filled with worry, and then she starts rambling about how we should split the work to do.

I hide a sigh of relief.

Nothing will happen between me and Lev—nothing dangerous nor sexual, despite what they seem to be convinced of. That's a matter of fact.

CHAPTER EIGHTEEN

When the doorbell rings, I jump up like I've just been electrocuted. Is he already here? I glance at the wall clock, my hands mechanically smoothing down the sides of my plaid skirt. We are to meet at eight o'clock—he's five minutes early. Lev strikes me as someone who deeply values punctuality, so this seems a bit out of character, but it doesn't bother me. Actually, I'm happy he's here early: I couldn't wait any longer. I check my reflection in the small mirror in the hallway, smoothing down the long, black strands of my hair, then I make my way to the door and I pull it open. My smile falters as soon as I realize Lev's not the one waiting outside. I push the door to try and close it, but Ben's quicker than me: he places one foot next to the doorframe, preventing me from locking myself inside.

"Now, now" he grunts, shoving the door with such strength I stumble backward, holding onto the wall to avoid a bad fall. "When did you become so fucking rude, huh?" He crosses the threshold of my apartment, not bothering to close the door behind him, and starts walking toward me. "Your boyfriend comes to pay you a visit and you try to slam the door in his face?"

"You're not my boyfriend and you're not welcome here" I reply, fighting to keep my voice stable. I point at the doorway.

"Go away. Now."

He doesn't listen: his steps are long and fast, and in a second, he reaches me. He grabs my elbow to pull me closer, his grip painful. There's a mad gleam lighting up his gaze. "A stripper?" he snorts, pushing me against the wall. "What fucking possessed you to accept?"

"Are you nuts?" I shout, pulling my arm free with a hard tug. "It's the job *you* found!"

He manages to grab me again, his fingers sinking in the tender flesh of my forearm. "I thought you'd be serving tables, not this!"

"Well, guess what: it's none of your business. Let go of me!" I pull and pull, but his grip is too strong—I'm only hurting myself. I can already see red marks blooming on the skin under his fingers. "Let go, you psycho!"

"Call her now" he frantically mumbles, his free hand searching my skirt pockets. "You call Kath immediately and quit, because she won't fucking fire you, even though I asked her nicely."

I move backward, but I only manage to trip on the carpet and fall, the couch barely breaking the tumble. Ben is on me in less than a second.

I blindly kick, knee, and scratch him, but he doesn't move, his whole weight pressing me down. "Stop, *stop!*" I shout, thrashing under him, trying to break free. "Let me go!"

"Not before you resign" he replies with a grunt, his hands pulling, searching, so intrusive they make me want to throw up. "Where's your phone?"

I don't think: I reach for it, buried deep in the back pocket of my skirt, and I throw it in Ben's face.

"Fucking bitch!" he shouts, his hands pressed on his nose. "That hurt!"

Taking advantage of his confusion, I scramble to slide away, crawling on the thin, wrinkled carpet. I'm too slow: in the span of one second, Ben is on me. He straddles my legs, pushes my face on the floor, and for a second, he just stops. I almost hear the wheels turning in his head, thinking, considering. I definitely hear his breath grow labored, feel him shift to sit in a more comfortable position, feel his gaze piercing my back.

"You're stuck, huh?" he hisses. There's a weird edge to his voice, an undertone that makes me shiver. "Bet you're not feeling so bold right now. No, you're vulnerable... at my mercy."

That said, he lifts the back of my skirt.

"No, no, no!" I scream when I realize what he's planning to do. "I'll call her, I'll... Whatever you want, but stop!"

"Too late" he rumbles, as he struggles to pull my thighs down. "Someone needs to show you how to fucking behave. You want to be a whore, I'll treat you like one. And let's be honest." He fumbles with his belt, then I hear a zipper coming undone. "It was about time. Two years of waiting... can you imagine? I've been a fucking saint."

I scream. I scream and kick and wriggle, but he doesn't budge: he just sits on me, keeping my head down, his free hand reaching for my underwear.

Part of me doesn't want to believe this is happening. It's clinging to the hope it's all just a bad dream, a horrible nightmare. And maybe, just maybe, if I shake myself hard enough, I'll be able to wake up—safe, unharmed, far away from him.

"Please, please, please" I sob, my voice barely recognizable. "Please, stop. We can talk about—"

I don't get to finish my sentence: one second he's squishing me down on the floor, the next he's gone, letting me breathe freely.

I roll on my back. Ben is being retained against the wall, his feet aimlessly kicking in mid-air, a hand wrapped around his throat holding him up. It belongs to a tall, dark-haired man towering over him, a man who closely resembles...

"Lev" I gasp, the second I recognize him.

He turns his head toward me, still holding Ben against the wall. His gaze is stained with worry. "One minute, baby. I'm killing this pathetic excuse of a human being and—"

"No" I stutter, using all I have left to stand up. "Lev, please, don't…" I move toward them, my steps uncertain, my legs unsteady. "I don't want you in jail because of him. Please."

He stiffens. His hand is still strangling Ben, now turning purple, struggling to breathe.

"Please" I repeat, and this time my voice cracks. I don't even try to hold back my tears: I'm too tired and frightened to care. "*Lev.*"

It seems to work: he gives Ben's throat one last squeeze, then he lets go, letting him tumble down on the floor. Ben scrambles to get himself back up, and with one last disoriented look in our direction, he runs out of the open door.

"I'm calling the police" Lev states, his voice tense, as he reaches for his phone. "Just give—"

I don't let him finish: I close the distance between us with one last step and bury my face in his chest, grabbing fistfuls of his sleeves to stop him. "Hold me" I sob, taking in his familiar, comforting scent. "Forget the police, just… just hold me. I need you. Please."

For a second, he doesn't do or say anything. I can barely feel his breath, coming out quick and sharp, caressing the crown of my head. Then he engulfs me in a tight hug, just the kind I need to keep it all together.

"Stay" I weep, as he picks me up. I tie my legs around his waist, my face sinking into his neck. "Don't let me go."

He holds me tighter, one hand on my back, the other under my butt. "Never" he whispers through my hair. "Not unless you want me to."

I shake my head, unable to say anything else. He's here, with me, and I'm safe: that's all that matters right now.

I barely register him kicking the door closed, taking a seat on the couch with my legs still wrapped around him, his hands pulling up my torn thighs. All I can focus on is his breath, his beating heart, his warmth enveloping me.

"I'm here" he murmurs, slowly stroking my back, placing

small kisses on my head. "I'm here with you, baby."

We stay like this for who knows how long, before I finally stop crying and start feeling like myself again. I raise my head, but I can't bring myself to look into Lev's eyes.

"Your pretty shirt is ruined" I sniff, staring at the wet patch on his shoulder. "I'm so sorry."

"Coral, look at me." He strokes my chin with his index finger, encouraging me to lift my head. His eyes carry a tenderness I'm not used to. "Do you think I care?"

I shrug. "I would. It looks expensive."

"It's a piece of clothing" he murmurs, his fingers wiping my wet cheeks. "An object. I couldn't care less, baby."

I should correct him, tell him it's inappropriate, but I can't bring myself to do it: the way he says *baby* is just so endearing and comforting.

"Thank you for what you did" I mumble, carefully avoiding his gaze. "And I'm sorry... I'm sorry for how I reacted. You know, I should probably..." I untie my legs, trying to push away from him, but he doesn't let go of my hips—so now I'm straight up straddling him. "I should get up. Give you some space."

For seemingly endless moments, he doesn't say anything. His eyes map out a slow path along my face, lingering on certain spots for longer, as if he were trying to engrave them into his mind. "Do me a favor" he says at last, his voice quiet. "Don't apologize. Not in a situation like this."

"But—"

"No" he interrupts me, grazing my lips with his knuckles. "It's fair to apologize when you do something wrong. This is not the case."

I have to resist the urge to kiss, lick, nibble at his smooth fingers. Instead, I take a deep breath and bite my lower lip. "I overreacted."

"You most definitely didn't" he replies, and a muscle in his jaw twitches. "If I hadn't arrived in time..."

"But you did" I remind him, cocking my head. "And I'm

fine. I'm just embarrassed I acted that way. Your presence..." I shake my head, looking down. "I felt like I needed to be physically close to you, to... you know, to calm down, and in fact it made me feel a thousand times better."

"I'd tell you the reason, but you made it clear you aren't willing to talk about it."

I guess this is about the mate thing. I'm not even surprised: the sudden need to be close to him has no logical explanation. At least, I can't find one.

"Who was that?" he asks, his voice as soft as his hands slowly caressing my back. "I have a feeling you already knew him."

I hold my breath for a second, my gaze searching Lev's. He may be acting calm, but there's a flickering rage half hidden in his dark irises. "Before I tell you, promise me you won't do anything."

His jaw stiffens. "He assaulted you. And something tells me it's not the first time."

"Still" I mumble, tracing one of his black buttons with the tip of my index fingernail. "I don't want you in jail because of him."

Lev chuckles, a low sound making his body vibrate under mine. "How naive."

"No, Lev." I raise my head, holding his intense stare. "I don't care about how powerful and rich you are. You won't put yourself in danger because of him."

He cocks an eyebrow. "Will you call the police?"

"I... It's complicated."

"How?"

I bite my lower lip, taking a deep breath. "He was my boyfriend. First and only. We met at a party about two years ago and immediately started dating, because..." I shrug. "I don't know. He made me feel pretty, I guess."

"Pretty?" He scoffs. "You're drop-dead gorgeous, Coral. Hope you know that."

I can feel myself blushing. "Well... I had just lost my mom.

I was completely on my own, besides a few friends, and he… he arrived at the right time. Distracted me with compliments and little gifts." My head sinks into my shoulders. "Now I realize he's always been a prick, disrespecting me and pushing me into doing things I… I wasn't comfortable with."

"It doesn't explain why you don't want to call the police" Lev murmurs, his long fingers tracing my jawline. "He was going to rape you. I don't want to force you to relive it, but I *do* want you to be safe."

"He was going to stop" I whisper, but I know it's a lie.

He shakes his head. "No. And I want him nowhere near you, so will you please call the police?"

I open my mouth just to close it again a second later, unsure about what to say. Ben *did* assault me: why am I so reticent to press charges? It's not because of what we used to have—as of right now, I couldn't care less. I wish I could erase those whole two years we were together, actually.

No, it's… it's different. The mere thought of going through the process of pressing charges is draining. I just want this thing to go away, for it to disappear into thin air, annihilated, as if it never even existed.

I know it won't, but it's a comforting thought, nonetheless.

"I just have so much going on" I mutter, snuggling against Lev's chest. "I'm tired. I don't want to deal with this too."

He draws little circles on my back, his warmth traveling through my thin shirt and tickling my skin. "You wouldn't be so tired if you let me take care of you."

I raise my head just enough to look at him. "You don't have to provide for me. I'm not your kid."

A sly smirk tugs his lips upwards. "You could still call me daddy."

"Lev!" I smack him in the chest, trying to hold in a laugh. "Never say that again. God, it was so bad."

He taps on my lower lip. "At least I made you laugh."

"It was a laugh of embarrassment" I point out, even though I'm still giggling. "So you can stop being all smug about it."

"Oh, never" he replies, his voice low and raspy, a hint of a smile hiding in his eyes. "Never." He looks at me, his gaze taking me in one inch at a time, then he sighs. "Please tell me you're considering calling the police."

"I, huh…" I bite my lips, retracting a bit. "I'll avoid him. Easy peasy."

"No." Lev shakes his head. "He knows where you live, and this place is a wreck. He could easily kick the door down."

"Then what do you want me to do?"

"Call the police" he articulates, his voice harsh and unwilling to compromise. "Press charges. I'll pay for a good lawyer, if it comes to it."

I take a long, deep breath, my heart beating fast inside my chest. "It would be useless. The police won't do anything about it."

Lev sits straighter, causing me to slide forward. My pussy, barely covered with thighs and underwear, rubs against him. He's rock hard under me.

He feels it too: he stiffens, his breath ragged, his eyes so dark I can't distinguish the pupil from the iris.

"Coral" he mutters, and I have to resist the urge to start rocking my hips back and forth. I bet it would feel heavenly. "You may want to back off a tad bit."

"I'm comfy here" I breathe, sinking deeper into his crotch. "And it's the perfect position, no?"

"For what?" he asks, his voice almost a growl.

"You still need to drink, remember?" I push myself closer, exposing my throat, and I can't resist circling my hips over his erection. "We both could use the bite."

Lev takes a deep breath, his eyes closed. When he finally looks at me, there's an unmistakable darkness in his gaze—desire, so wild and primordial it makes me want to rip his clothes off, then have him rip mine off, and then…

"I'm not feeding off you after what happened" he says, popping my little bubble of delight. "You went through enough as it is."

"No, I'm fine" I argue, sitting upright as if that could convince him. "It's not like he injured me."

Lev shakes his head. "First off, he did." His fingers brush over my forearm, where angry red marks color my otherwise pale skin. "But I wasn't even talking about that. I'm not taking advantage of you after such a traumatic experience. I can wait, Coral." And the way he says it, I swear that simple sentence carries more than one meaning.

"If you really don't want to alert the police, at least come stay at my place."

I let out an obnoxious laugh. "Excuse me, what?"

"You heard me" he says, his expression completely serious. "Keep in mind you signed a contract."

"What… What's that got to do with it?" I ask, shaking from laughter.

"You promised to take care of yourself for the duration of the contract." Lev cocks an eyebrow. "This is *not* taking care of yourself. What if something happens to you?"

I part my lips, but I can't make a single sound other than a strangled, a bit hysterical half-laugh. "So that's what you're worried about? That you could lose your expensive blood bag?"

"Obviously not" he answers, his voice so tense with rage it almost trembles. "But you don't like when I talk about my feelings for you, so I'm trying to make you reason in some other way."

"It'll be fine" I mumble, carefully avoiding the 'feelings' part. "I can look after myself."

Lev holds my gaze for two, three, four seconds, then he nods, a glint of defeat in his eyes. "I know you can. That doesn't mean I don't want to protect you."

I hold my breath. There's a part of me who's screaming to just give in, but I silence it.

"It'll be fine" I repeat, forcing myself to smile. "I promise."

If I could only believe that.

CHAPTER NINETEEN

Over the next few weeks, I fall into a sort of nice, predictable routine. If I have class, I wake up at seven, shower, get ready, and grab breakfast with Sasha and Piper at the little café just outside Lehman University. If I don't, I sleep in, then I clean my apartment and go for a walk.

I haven't heard from Ben since that night. He hasn't tried to reach out in any way or ambush me, I haven't found him following me around. Which is great. Weird, but great anyway. Part of me still feels a bit unsafe, still expects to see him jump out of every corner, but I'm almost fully convinced Lev scared him off for good.

Talking about Lev, he calls me every two days to fulfill his needs. That overpowering feeling I get when he bites me hasn't subsided one bit. If anything, it's growing stronger by the day. Anyhow, despite me telling him I can go to him just fine, he's always the one coming to me—whether I'm home, at uni, hanging out with my friends or at the club.

He hasn't stopped booking me the whole night, by the way. Every time I have a shift, I get sent directly to his favorite room (or so I assume, since it's the only one he requests), where I spend the entire night working on assignments, studying, squirming a bit under Lev's intense stare. He's not always there, though: sometimes he's busy with work stuff, so I just spend my shift all alone in the empty VIP room, studying and trying to convince myself that ache in my chest has nothing to do with Lev not being there.

That's what I'm doing tonight: reading half a sentence, checking my phone to see if there are any new notifications, fidgeting with my highlighters without getting anything done. Truth is I'm expecting a text from Lev. He said there was a chance he could be here for the last half hour of my shift, feed off me and drive me home—my car is inoperable: it has a flat tire, but I haven't had time to change it, so I've been moving around on foot all day long.

I check my phone for the umpteenth time, but he hasn't written anything.

Come on, just say you'll make it.

I'm trying to persuade myself that if I'm this anxious over a stupid text is just because I'm too tired to go back home on foot, but deep down, I know better: it's not about this. In case he can't get here in time, he'll send his chauffeur to drive me home—I'm covered no matter what. The actual reason I'm hoping he'll text me saying he got off earlier is just that I want to see him.

I'll never admit it, though.

I sigh, making the highlighter rotate between my fingers, and I force myself to focus.

Lev sends a message right at the end of my shift, while I'm getting changed into warmer clothes, and I get immediately disappointed.

I can't make it, Coral, I'm sorry. My driver is getting to you, he'll take you home safely. Please, wait for him inside and only go out when he calls you—I gave him your number. See you soon.

I write a quick response to thank him, trying to hide my sadness with too many exclamation marks.

I shouldn't feel this way, I tell myself, as I gather my things from the locker. It's not… It's not appropriate, to say the least. But as much as my rational self is convinced of this, there's a part of me who simply refuses to accept the decision. It forces me to think about how it would be, what a relationship with Lev would mean in my life, how the two of us could make a nice couple. It pushes me to reflect on the way he treats me, makes me feel appreciated, listened to, seen. It makes me wonder if there's a way for us to be together, him being immortal and all of that. A few days ago, I was on the verge of searching for solutions on the internet, but at the last moment I turned off my computer. I can't afford to indulge in this type of thoughts—I swore I'd never fall for this shit again, and I fully intend to stay true to my word.

Despite Lev's advice (well, it was more of an order, even though he said please) to wait inside, I need some air, so I push the backdoor open and walk into the almost empty parking lot. It was a slow night—or so I've heard from the girls in the changing room.

Lev's driver isn't here yet, so I start walking around, trying to warm up a bit. It's a cold night, but the air smells clean and I can see a few stars dotting the sky. I don't want to go back inside.

I walk the length of the building, up to the corner which leads to a dark passage, then I turn around with a little swirl, ready to return to the starting point.

I walk one step before a hand grabs the hood of my coat, pulling me back. The choked noise I let out is swallowed by my frantic backward steps, as I try to stay upright.

"Stop!" I cry, but the sound is muffled by a hand covering my mouth.

I immediately recognize the smell of the skin pressed against my face. More than two years with a person will do that to you.

Ben tries to drag me into the dark alley, but I can't let him: I don't even want to think about what he'd do to me if he were to succeed.

I bite hard into his palm, and he pulls his hand away, muttering a curse word under his breath. I don't waste any time: I unzip my coat and slip out of it, then I run. I need to get inside, I need to…

"You bitch, that hurt" he growls, grabbing a fistful of my hair.

I'm yanked back, the pain in my scalp so unbearable, for a second I fail to think straight.

"Oh, but you're going to pay" he says, dragging me toward the building's corner. "You're going to pay for *everything*."

I struggle to get free, but he's still pulling my ponytail, while his free hand is tightly wrapped around my waist. His grip is too strong.

I scream as the darkness from the alley closes onto me, making it hard to see. I wriggle and wave my arms and cry out for help, but it's all useless—Ben pushes my head forward and I hit the wall with my face. I can feel the skin over my right eyebrow split open, a warm liquid dripping down my forehead. It ends up in my eye, completely blinding me.

"No, stop" I screech, the pain a burning, pulsating red. "Leave me alone!"

He doesn't. His hands are all over me, his breath warm and humid against my exposed neck, his presence invading and pushy.

I realize then and there I need to get free. If I don't, he won't stop at raping me—he'll do something irreversible, something I won't be able to recover from.

I turn around, still blind from the darkness and the blood dripping in my eye, and I try to kick him. I miss a few times, but then I hit him—and I hit him hard, given the screech he lets out. I don't stop: I just kick and kick until he takes a step back, and then I shove him out of the way, running toward the lights.

The blood is a pinkish, watery veil in my eyes, but I see the outline of a black car parked in front of the building just fine.

Lev's chauffeur.

I push forward, giving him a wave, dragging my heavy

limbs across the parking lot. "Please, I..."

He sees me. Thank goodness, he sees me, and he rushes out the car to get to me. He asks questions, examines my wounds, but I don't really follow.

"Ben" I mutter, my tongue swollen and heavy in my mouth. "He's... I think he's still back there."

"I'll take you to the hospital, alright?"

I shake my head no. "I don't need the hospital. I just... I just want to see Lev."

"I'll promptly call him, but you need to..."

And I know he says something else, but I don't listen. Not because I don't want to—I just can't. It's like one second I'm there, the next I'm sinking in a pool of darkness that has nothing to do with the fact it's nighttime.

Part of me knows I should fight to resurface, but I don't want to.

I just let myself sink.

CHAPTER TWENTY

When I open my eyes, I'm lying on a hospital bed and there's a needle sticking out of my left arm. It's connected to a long tube traveling up high to a plastic bag, held up by a long metal pole.

I'm a bit confused and my throat is dry, but besides that, I'm fine. I'm not even in pain.

"Coral."

I turn my head. Lev is getting up from a chair, a worried glint in his eyes. "Huh, hi" I mumble, trying to sit up.

He pushes me back down, tucking me in. "How do you feel? Wait, let me call someone, first."

"I'm fine" I reply, as I try to sit up again. "I'm not in pain."

"Please, stay still. What if…"

"I'm okay, Lev. Seriously." I rearrange the pillows behind my back to better support me, then I give him a quick glance. "I, huh… well. How are you?"

Lev blinks, coking an eyebrow. "How am I?"

"I mean, yeah." I nod, shrugging. "Am I not allowed to ask?"

"Coral, you've been assaulted again by that scumbag" he says, frowning. "My driver found you wandering through the parking lot, bloody and confused. You shouldn't be the one asking me how I am."

I bite my lip. "Well, I want to know."

"I'm relieved to see you're okay" he sighs, sitting back down on the chair. Then he glowers at me, his lips a thin line. "And I'm mad."

"At me?"

"At you, at him, at the whole fucking world." He looks controlled, but his voice is cracking a bit. "I thought I'd lost you."

My heart is beating so fast I'm scared he will hear it. "You were right" I mutter, lowering my head. "I'll go to the police. I'll go to the police and press charges, I promise."

"It won't be necessary" he says, reaching out to brush a strand of my hair back. "He's already in jail. A security camera filmed the entire thing, start to finish." His jaw stiffens, and a glimmer of rage lights up his eyes. "You'll need to make a statement, and there will be a trial, but it's a formality. There's video evidence he did this to you."

"Really?" I stupidly ask.

Lev nods. "You don't need to worry about anything, baby."

I don't even get the urge to correct him. Why would I? I want to be his baby, and I don't want to waste any more time. I've realized just how quickly things can change, and I don't want to lose him. I can't.

A doctor with long, black braids walks in to check on me. She asks some questions, then proceeds to tell me that I just have a few scratches and bruises, and that I can go home, but I need to rest for a while.

"I'm sure your husband will take good care of you" she says, before flashing a smile and backing out of the room.

"Husband?" I repeat, turning to face him. "Am I missing something?"

He shrugs. "They wouldn't let me in."

"We don't even have rings" I giggle, raising my left hand. "How did you manage to convince them?"

Lev gives me a sly, lazy grin, leaning over me. "It's a secret." He brushes my jawline with his warm knuckles. "She was right, though. I will take good care of you."

"You better" I warn him, trying to hold back a laugh. "I expect nothing less from my fake husband."

"Trust me, Coral" he mumbles, so close I can feel his breath on my mouth. "You won't be disappointed."

CHAPTER
TWENTY-ONE

Lev refused to let me go home, insisting I would need assistance, so now I'm at his loft. He only agreed to stop by at my apartment to let me grab some clothes and toiletries.

"I had the bed changed before we arrived" he explains, setting my bags on the dresser. "So it's clean for you to sleep in."

I open my mouth and then close it again, slightly shaking my head.

"What?" he asks, stepping directly in front of me. "Something wrong?"

"I, huh…" I nod toward the fluffy-looking bed. "What about you? Where are you going to sleep?"

A wide grin stretches his lips. "You thought we'd share a bed?"

"We already did. Besides, I doubt you'd be comfortable on the couch."

He takes a step forward, still smiling. "There's a spare bedroom."

"Oh, uhm… Well, good to know" I mumble, pretending to be busy with my bags.

"Coral?"

"Mhhh?"

His warmth spreads across my back. He's not touching

me, but I can feel how close he is. "I can stay, if you want me to."

I stop fumbling, a shiver traveling through my body.

"Not to fuck" he mumbles, his voice raspy. "I just want to hold you."

I slowly turn around, my heart beating fast as I face him. "What if… What if I want to?"

"For me to stay?" Lev asks, as his gaze caresses my figure.

"For you to fuck me."

Crap, I can't believe I've actually said that. It's just… I want him closer, closer, closer, I crave his touch, I want to feel him in every way possible.

Lev cocks an eyebrow. "Language."

"You said it first" I point out.

"Fair enough." He shakes his head, his hands delicately resting on my hips. "But no. We're not fucking tonight. Your last twenty-four hours have been rough, baby. You need to rest."

I open my mouth to tell him it doesn't matter, that I want him right now and that I can't wait any longer, but I hesitate. I *do* need to rest. And most of all, I don't want to associate our first night together with the horrible experience I've had with Ben.

"Then can we cuddle?" I quietly ask, looking at him with pleading eyes. "Just cuddle."

He draws me closer to him and kisses my collarbone, barely exposed by the boat neck of my t-shirt. "Of course we can, if that's what you want."

I nod, and that's all it takes for him to scoop me in his arms and carry me to bed.

Under the blankets, we face each other, close and yet not nearly enough. That's why I push myself toward him until I can feel the warmth of his body engulfing me. It's the safest I've ever felt in my entire life.

"Hi" I whisper, resting my head on his pillow.

A smirk curves his lips upwards. "Hi. Everything alright?"

"Yeah." I nod, slowly caressing his toned chest. I can feel how warm and solid he is even through the thick fabric of his t-shirt. "I just need you close."

Lev doesn't answer: he wraps his arms around me and drags me closer, until our chests are pressed together and I can feel his slow, steady heartbeat.

"Enough?" he murmurs, his breath tickling the tip of my nose.

It never feels enough, with him, but I keep it to myself and simply nod. "Thank you."

"For what?"

"Everything" I reply, my voice barely above a whisper. "Being here. Taking care of me. Being so patient."

He places a small, delicate kiss on my temple. "Always." There's a moment of silence before he takes a deep breath. "I'm sorry I wasn't there to protect you."

"I'm sorry I didn't listen to you" I whisper back, hiding my face in the spot where his neck and shoulder meet. His scent is heavenly. "You were right."

His fingers draw lines up my back, while his free hand strokes my hair. "The only thing I care about is that you're okay. The rest is meaningless." His chest expands with a deep breath. "I often find myself fantasizing about turning you."

"Into a vampire?" I stupidly ask, even though I already know the answer.

"You'd be stronger" he mutters. "Safer for when I'm not around."

I tilt my head back to look at him. "Wouldn't my blood change?"

Lev cocks an eyebrow. "And?"

"You like my blood" I whisper, unsure. "And if I were a vampire... Wouldn't our contract be invalid?"

He has a pensive look on his face as he slowly caresses my jawline. "The contract is already invalid, Coral. It was a mere mean to try and get you closer." He leans in, his lips pressing an excruciatingly slow line of kisses up my neck. "Besides...

We'd drink from each other."

I barely suppress a laugh. "Is that a thing? I thought it was just a cheesy ruse used in TV shows."

"It's not" he murmurs, an amused edge to his words. "It's very much real… and pleasurable for both parts."

I feel my cheeks grow warmer at the thought of how his bites make me feel. "Yeah?"

"Yeah."

We keep quiet for a little, merely enjoying each other's proximity, the slow exploring of our hands. It's only a while later, when my back is resting against his broad chest, that I feel the urge to ask him some questions.

"Were you turned?"

There's a moment of silence behind me, Lev's torso stiffening for a split second before relaxing again. "I was born like this. My parents were turned in the epidemic."

"Are you close with them?"

There's another second of hesitation before he answers, "Not exactly."

I nod while lightly scratching his arm, wrapped around me. "Is this a sensitive topic? We can talk about something else or—"

"It's perfectly fine" he interrupts me, then he kisses the back of my head. "Ask away, baby."

"Did something happen between you and your parents?" I murmur, exploring his long fingers with mine. "You don't have to answer, if you don't want to."

Behind me, Lev takes a deep breath. I think he's about to ask me to shut up, but I couldn't be more wrong: he starts opening up a bit about his past.

"They believe vampires to be a superior race" he sighs, as his big hand fans under my t-shirt, searching the skin of my stomach. The thumb is brushing the lower part of my breast, a light touch that manages to make me squirm, nonetheless. "They undervalue human beings, consider them on a par with… well, walking blood dispensers."

His words make me tense up a little, even though I'm aware many vampires feel that way.

"They did things I cannot condone" he goes on, his voice grave. "So I cut them off. I left the community around fifty years ago and tried to build something for myself."

"And you did" I whisper, squeezing his hand. "Do you miss them?"

"Sometimes" he admits, a hint of vulnerability filtering though his words. "But it's fine. I made my choice, and they surely didn't try to stop me. We were too different."

I caress his forearm in slow, rhythmic strokes. "You were really brave to walk away."

For a second he stays quiet, fingers gently drumming on my stomach. "Why these questions?" he asks softly.

I bite my lower lip. "Did I make you uncomfortable?"

"Not at all." He pushes my hair out of the way and licks the sensitive spot behind my ear, making me shiver. "I was curious. Are you thinking about letting me turn you?"

The question makes me go stiff. It's not that I haven't thought about it, but it's so… so sudden. I don't know if I'm ready to make such a final decision. Vampires don't die of natural causes, and the possibility of living forever scares me shitless.

"I don't know" I murmur. "It's scary. I guess… I guess I need to think about it."

"Take your time, baby." He adjusts his position to pull me even closer, and my butt rubs against him. He's rock hard, and yet he still refused to fuck me, putting my needs before everything else. "Whatever your decision may be, I'll be here for as long as you want. Now rest, yeah?"

I bite my lips, squirming in his arms to turn around. "I don't think I can sleep."

In the semidarkness, I can barely make out his confused scowl. "Is something bothering you?"

"Your cock" I whisper, holding back a laugh. "It's poking my back and butt. I'll wake up full of bruises, if we don't do something about it."

His body stiffens, his breath getting ragged. "Coral…"

"I'm not talking about fucking" I reassure him, caressing his jaw. "Can I… Is it okay if I touch you?"

"Touch me how?" he asks, his voice raspy and dangerously low. "Be specific, baby."

I only hesitate for a second before straddling his legs, leaving enough room to get access to his groin in case he says yes. "I, huh… I want to touch you cock" I admit, my eyes on the bulge stretching his pants. "Make you feel good. Is it okay?"

"Are you really asking?"

"Consent is important" I whisper, biting my lip. "Can I touch you, Lev?"

He rubs his face with his fingers, then reaches out to pull me down toward him. "Touch me, kiss me, destroy me" he groans, inches away from my lips. "I'm at your mercy. I've been from the very beginning."

This is all I need: I sit back up, my hands feeling him through the fabric of his sweatpants. "You're big" I say, rubbing his cock with my flattened hand. "So big and hard."

"This is what you do to me" he mutters, shuddering under my touch. "Do you see how powerful you are?"

"I feel powerful" I reply, as I take his cock out. He's even bigger than I thought while touching him through his pants. I close my hand around the base and lightly squeeze, feeling the bulging veins press against my skin. His body tenses in response. "Very powerful."

It's the truth: seeing Lev, usually so composed and stiff, twitching and panting under my touch is somewhat intoxicating.

I lean in, letting a trickle of saliva pour on the swollen, pink head. I spread it all over his length, then I start stroking him—slowly, up and down, my grip firm around him.

"Fucking hell" he hisses, rocking his hips up and up. "You're killing me, baby. I won't last long."

"Then I better hurry." I slide back a little and bow down,

placing a small kiss on the tip of his hot cock. "I want to swallow something of yours, too."

I lick him, one long stroke from base to tip, the veins tickling my flattened tongue. I twirl it around the head and lick the drop of precum glistening on the tip, Lev's moans vibrating though me. I slide his cock in my mouth, letting it stretch my lips wide open to try and take as much as possible. It's salty and absolutely delicious. It's not my first time doing this, but it surely it's the first time I'm enjoying it.

Lev rocks his hips toward my face, his rhythm erratic, almost frantic, desperate for release, making me feel like a goddess. The powerful and intimidating vampire is a quivering mess under my kisses—I'm afraid I'm going to get addicted to it.

"Do you like it?" I breathe, before drawing a long line of kisses down his shaft. "Do you like how my mouth feels on you?"

"Coral, please" he begs in a choked voice. "Please."

I suck on his swollen balls as I massage his cock with both of my hands, stroking it fast, hard. I can't get enough of his moans, of the way he's rocking under me. It makes me want to touch myself to satisfy the growing itch between my legs.

"Like that" he pants, when I vacuum the head of his cock in my mouth, sucking hard. "Please, don't stop, don't…"

The rest of the sentence is consumed by a low moan, and warm, thick cum fills my mouth.

I swallow it all, ending my blowjob by licking every inch of his cock clean.

"Fucking hell" Lev breathes, pulling me to him. His eyes, still dark with arousal, search mine. "You're good."

"Only for you." I wet my lips, still tasting like him, and lean in for a kiss. I softly bite his lower lip. "You taste good." I stare at him for a second, unspeaking, then I crack a small smile. "Now we can sleep." I give him another peck on the lips and snuggle on my side, wrapping his arm around me. "Goodnight, Lev."

CHAPTER
TWENTY-TWO

When I open my eyes, the buttery and soft light that precedes dawn softens the hard lines and edges of the room… including the ones of the man—pardon, the vampire— propped up on his elbow to stare at me.

"Creepy" I manage, my voice gritty. "You don't stare at people while they're sleeping. Red flag."

He brushes a strand of messy hair away from my face, his hand lingering on my right cheek. "You haunted my dreams all night, so it's only fair. How do you feel?"

"A bit sore" I admit, brushing the plaster on my forehead. "But fine. Really. How are you?"

"I spent the night with the woman I love in my arms" he murmurs, as he pulls me closer. "I'm over the moon, Coral."

Love. I already knew, but hearing him say it out loud, so directly, makes my heart flutter. "I'm happy too" I whisper, looking down at the mess of sheets on the bed. "I can't remember the last time I've been this happy, to be honest."

"I'm glad." Lev leans forward and kisses my jawline, his mouth soft and warm. "Last night you gave me the orgasm of my life and not even three minutes later you were snoring like a truck." He gently bites the soft flesh under my jaw. "You didn't even give me the chance to reciprocate. You'll find I'm not a selfish lover" he murmurs in between kisses, covering the skin of my throat in goosebumps. "Quite the contrary."

"Oh" I hum, feeling my face getting hot. "Good to know."

He places a hand on my chest and softly pushes me down on the mattress. "If you let me, I'll show you."

I sharply inhale, heart hammering in my chest. His dark gaze alone is making me tingle in places I believed to be dead and buried. "It's not... It's not necessary" I stutter, my voice croaky. "You don't have to do it just because last night I—"

"How naive" he interrupts me in a murmur. "Do you really believe I'm not consumed by the idea of suffocating between your legs?"

The night has taken away part of my audacity, so his words kind of make me want to hide, but I'm still enthralled. "I don't know?"

"I'll enlighten you, then." Starting from my throat, he leaves a trail of kisses that cover my heaving chest, my stomach, my lower belly. "I want to bury my tongue deep inside your cunt. Feel you squirm as I suck on your clit, rub it with my fingers, nibble on it." His lips linger just above the hem of my pajama shorts. "I want to taste your orgasm, watch you lose your mind under the laps of my tongue."

A ghost of a smile curves his lips up as he entirely avoids my genital area, placing the next kiss on my inner thigh, instead.

"Please" I mumble, pushing my hips closer to him.

"Please what?" He cocks an eyebrow. "You said it yourself last night. Consent is important, and I wholeheartedly agree."

I hold back a desperate whine. "Do it, *please*. Everything you just said. Eat me out, make me *come*."

A sly grin stretches his mouth as he hooks the hem of my shorts with his fingers, slowly pulling them down. "Now we're talking."

He's lying on his stomach, his face a few inches away from my pussy. He rubs his nose over my cotton panties, then places a chaste kiss on them "I bet your cunt tastes just as your blood does." He glances at me with a mischievous glint in his eyes, before proceeding to lower my underwear. "Heavenly."

He loops his arms around my legs, dragging me closer, and suddenly his tongue is on me. It slowly laps the area around the labia, drawing long, lazy lines, then it lightly brushes my clit, making me clench.

"Oh" I whimper, squirming on the mattress. My movements are limited by his strong grip, so I can't back off.

"You like it there?" he says, before circling it with his tongue. "Talk to me, baby. Tell me how you like it."

"There" I moan, letting my head roll back. "Right there."

"There what? Give me clear instructions. Want me to lick it?" He laps it with his flattened tongue, excruciatingly slow. "Suck on it?" He covers my clit with his mouth and starts sucking.

I let out a loud whine, arching my back. The intensity of it all is taking away my sanity. "Suck on it, and then… then…" A wave of pleasure passes through me, leaving me breathless for a couple of seconds. "Fuck" I moan, my hands gripping the sheets. "Lick it. Lick, suck, all of it."

As he shows me just how good he is with his tongue, I can feel this thing growing inside of me, pulsating, hot, taking up all the space in my body. My pussy pulses under Lev's intense laps, which are getting quicker, more demanding, erasing everything outside his tongue and the orgasm building deep down.

And then it happens: my body tenses up as the *thing* explodes in a wave of warmth and breathtaking contractions in my pussy, ripping a cry of pure bliss from my throat. I grab Lev's hair to push his head between my legs, rocking my hips to ride the wave of pleasure until the very last drop.

"Oh my god" I pant, as my body finally relaxes. Now I feel like a puddle, a very satisfied one. "Oh my god. That was… intense."

Lev kisses his way up my stomach, chest, and neck, then playfully bites my throat without piercing the skin. "I was right" he murmurs, rubbing his nose along my jawline. "You taste heavenly."

"Do you... Do you want to drink?" I ask, still breathless from my very first orgasm. An earth-shattering one, too. "I mean, my blood."

He looks at me with a gentleness in his eyes so intense I can almost feel it caressing me. "Not right now. I've weakened you enough, haven't I?"

I lift my head to kiss him, his mouth hot on mine. My taste is still on his lips. "Not at all. Please?" I bite my lower lip. "If I decide to let you turn me, maybe it won't be the same anymore."

His gaze is gentle on me, but there's a hint of anticipation in it. "Are you considering it?"

"Maybe" I reply, my voice weak. "It's just scary. And big."

"I can imagine how you feel." Lev's fingers slip under my t-shirt, gripping my right hip. "There's no rush to decide."

I nod, keeping quiet. I can't see myself with anyone but him, romantically speaking, but it's still a lot.

"How about we start small?" he murmurs, still exploring my body under the t-shirt. "Dating, getting to know each other..."

"Not living together until I can pay for shared expenses" I chime in, trying to hold back a smile. "It sounds good."

He frowns and drags me closer. "That's not an issue."

"I don't want to live off of you. Speaking of which," I say, glancing at the alarm clock on Lev's nightstand, "I have class today."

He lets me sit up, but doesn't look particularly happy about it. "You were badly injured."

"I barely have a few scratches" I murmur, before giving him a quick kiss on the corner of his mouth. "I'm fine. Your tongue made me dizzier than Ben slamming my head against the wall. I'm really fine, Lev."

"The doctor said you should rest" he insists, as he pushes my hair behind my ears. "I don't want you to feel worse because you didn't listen."

I kiss him again, then push myself back to get off the bed and retrieve some clean clothes. "It'll be okay. If I get tired, I'll go home… *my* home" I clarify, quickly putting on a pair panties. "I want to be with you, but living together is a big deal. I need some time, and I imagine it wouldn't be easy for you to share your spaces with me so suddenly."

"It would" he replies, not a hint of hesitation in his words. "It would be easy, Coral, because I want nothing more than spending the rest of eternity with you." He gets up as well, slowly making his way toward me. "What is sharing a space when I want to share my entire life?"

My breath catches in my throat. "Oh. Uhm."

"My wish doesn't have to be yours" he replies, walking up to me. He leans in, resting his hand on the small of my back, inches above the curve of my ass. "I don't expect it. I've had hundreds of years to get used to the idea of having a partner for the entirety of my existence, but you didn't." He brushes my neck with his lips. "I'm willing to wait. I'm willing to let you go, if that's what you desire. But please, don't simply assume to know what I want or don't want to try and voice your own worries."

I'm speechless and barely react when he kisses me. Okay, he's kind of right, but I still wasn't expecting him to say it so directly.

I'll have to get used to his openness.

CHAPTER TWENTY-THREE

Piper and Sasha are waiting for me outside the American literature classroom, and as I was expecting, the first thing Piper notices is the plaster sticking to forehead. "Oh my god, what happened to your head?"

Sasha notices something else, instead. "Who cares! Look at her, she finally got laid." She snickers. "Was it the vampire? I've heard they're godlike in bed."

I can feel myself blush. "I did not get laid."

"You most definitely did" she replies, a knowing smile curving her lips. "And the dick was apparently really good. Look at that smile!"

"Shhh!" I shush her, frantically looking around. The hallway is packed with people, but nobody seems to be paying attention to us. Still. I'm not really into sharing my sex life with a bunch of strangers. "Not here" I say, adjusting the strap of my bag. "Let's go somewhere else."

We head to the cafeteria for lunch, but since it's quite early, the place is almost empty.

"So, was it him?" Sasha asks, as we make our way to our usual table. "The vampire?"

"He has a name" I mumble, placing down the tray. "Lev. And… Well, we didn't go all the way, actually."

"But you did do something." Sasha flashes a grin and elbows Piper, sitting next to her. "Finally we found someone to show her there's a whole world beyond shitty Ben."

I can't help it: at the sound of his name, I flinch. For a while it was easy to pretend nothing happened, especially while I was in Lev's arms—safe. But now the memory is so vivid I have to stop and remind myself he can't hurt me anymore.

"Hey, you okay?" Piper asks, her voice soft.

I consider not telling them. It would be useless, since he's in jail and can't get to me anymore, but at the last moment I decide against it. I really need to get this off my chest.

"It was him. Ben." I point at the plaster, then I roll up my sleeves to show them the bruises staining my skin a deep purple. "A couple of days ago. A security camera recorded him... attacking me, so he's in jail now." I roll the sleeves back down. "I was in the hospital for around a day, they had to monitor me for twenty-four hours because of my head, but I'm sturdier than I look." I force out a small laugh. "After class I have to go to the police to give a statement... You know, about what happened. Lev is taking me."

As expected, my friends invest me with questions and curses directed at Ben, which I totally support. I try to explain everything in detail as we eat, and I find that letting it all out is kind of freeing.

I describe what happened when he showed up at my place, how Lev intervened and begged me to go to the police, and how I regrettably ignored him. I tell them about the night of the attack outside the Lust at first bite, the fear I felt in my bones, the thought I wouldn't make it out alive, how I blacked out not because of my injuries, but out of tension and fear leaving my body when I saw Lev's driver waiting for me.

"I'm glad you're okay" Piper says, even though I can tell she's kind of mad at me for not taking any measures against Ben. She keeps it to herself, though, and I'm grateful about it. I don't think I'd be able to endure a lecture, even if I know damn well I deserve it.

"And I'm glad that scumbag is in jail" Sasha adds, lifting her water flask as if she were making a toast. "May he rot in there for all eternity."

"Amen to that." Piper leans forward and clinks their bottles together, then she turns to face me. "So… You and Lev. Is this serious?"

I shrug as I feel my cheeks heat up. "Sort of. I think. I mean, I really like him, and he likes me too." I lower my gaze. "He's proved it to me. I want to take things slowly, though" I add, piling the empty dishes in my tray. "Dating, getting to know each other a bit better…"

"Letting him rearrange your insides" Sasha chimes in, barely holding in a snicker. "Yeah, we know the drill."

Piper playfully shoves her, then turns to me with a small smile, pushing her big curls away from her face. "I know I said some pretty bad things in the past, and I still kind of feel that way toward vampires, but… you seem happy. And as long as he doesn't do anything to harm you, I'm happy as well."

The conversation turns to our trip to New York, which is happening sooner than I thought: we're leaving in a couple of days. I've totally lost track of time in the past few weeks.

Luckily the trip is happening on the weekend, so we don't need to worry about class. I only have to ask for leave at the club… and tell Lev about it.

CHAPTER TWENTY-FOUR

Giving a statement to the police wasn't as tough as I thought it was going to be. A nice police officer sat me down in a small room with no windows, offered me something to drink, and then asked a few questions about my relationship with Ben, and especially on what had happened on that night. It only took about twenty minutes, then she escorted me back outside, where Lev was waiting for me.

Now he's driving toward my apartment, the car slowed down by the traffic, his right hand on my knee. "Are you sure you're okay?"

"Yeah" I reply softly. "It wasn't easy to relive it, but it's over. I'm fine." I run my fingers over his hand. "Thanks for taking me. How was your day?"

"Stressful" he sighs, eyes on the road ahead. "I'm dealing with a tough company acquisition and it's driving me insane." He briefly turns to me, his lips pointing upwards in a mischievous grin. "Now I'm better, though."

"I'm glad."

"What about you?" he then asks, as he squeezes my knee. "How was your day?"

This is the perfect chance to tell him about the trip. "All good. Class was okay, and I had lunch with my friends. They're eager to meet you." I clear my throat, biting the inside of my cheek. "Speaking of them… In a few days it will be Piper's birthday. Her mom gifted her a mini trip to New York, and I'm going, too."

"New York?" he repeats after me, giving me a quick glance. "It's a nice gift."

"It is" I agree, a small smile blooming on my lips. "And I'm glad to be spending some time with my friends. We've been kind of drifting apart because of busy schedules and such, so it's a good opportunity to reconnect."

Lev drums his fingers on the steering wheel, staring thoughtfully ahead. "I see. Where will you be staying?"

"Oh, uhm…" I dig up my phone from the bag and check Piper's last email, containing my plane tickets and a copy of the hotel reservation. "It's a youth hostel. Nothing fancy, but we'll be out exploring the city most of the time, so it's great."

"A youth hostel?" he asks, a dubious edge to his voice.

"One of those cheap places you book when you're young, broke and eager to travel" I explain, trying to hold back a laugh. "You often share rooms and bathrooms to save some money."

There's a moment of silence before he says, "I'll upgrade your accommodation."

"What?" This time I don't even try to hide my laughter. "No. There's no need."

"There is" he replies, not as amused as I am. "I don't like the idea of you sharing a room with strangers. Or a bathroom" he adds, slowly articulating each letter. "Something could happen to you."

"Something could happen to me anywhere, at any given time" I reply, arching an eyebrow. "Even now. Besides, I'm only sharing the room with my friends. Piper's mom booked a triple room just for the three of us."

He looks at me for a moment, but he averts his eyes so quickly I can't read his stare. "You'd be putting yourself in a dangerous situation. A perfectly avoidable one, too."

"Just because a place is cheap, it doesn't mean it's danger-

160

ous" I try to reason with him, ignoring the irritation surging up in my chest. "I'll be okay."

It's like I haven't spoken, because he goes on, "I'm upgrading your accommodation. End of story."

"You're upgrading absolutely nothing" I reply, a laughter of disbelief hidden behind my words. "This is a gift from my best friend's mom, and she was kind enough to include me as well, paying for me. You're not going to offend her or embarrass me, okay?"

Lev cocks an eyebrow. "How would it offend her?"

"You'd be basically saying what she was able to afford is not good enough" I explain, trying to stay calm in front of his arrogant obliviousness. "I'm not letting you. I'll stay in that youth hostel, whether you like it or not."

"Let's think this through" he insists, stopping at a red light. "What if I talked to your friend's mom? I could tell her this upgrade is a good thing for the three of you. You'd be staying in a nicer, safer hotel. How does the Waldorf-Astoria sound? It's on Park Avenue. You'd be well connected to safely explore the city."

I shake my head. "No. You'd offend her."

He restarts the car as soon as the light turns green, his big hands gripping the wheel. "You don't know. She could be happy about it."

"Maybe" I blurt out, fed up with his insistence. "Maybe not. You're absolutely right, I don't know. What I *do* know is that I don't want you to upgrade the fucking hotel. Is that clear?"

He doesn't look at me, but I see him clenching his jaw. "I'm not letting you stay somewhere unsafe."

"Lev, you're not my father" I articulate. "I've never had one, and I certainly don't need one now. Stop trying to boss me around."

"I just want you to be safe" he replies, a frustrated edge to his words. "How is that me trying to boss you around?"

I take a deep breath, trying to ease the rage burning inside me. Throwing a tantrum wouldn't help. "I've been looking after myself ever since my mom died, and I've been doing a damn good job, if you ask me."

"Coral, please." Lev takes a deep breath, eyes on the road unrolling in front of the car. The traffic is finally starting to clear up. "I've never said you can't look after yourself."

"You're implying it" I point out. "It's obvious. Don't try to deny it."

The car finally comes to a stop in front of my apartment building, and Lev turns to properly face me. "You've had a tough life, baby. Is it such an awful thing that I want to take care of you?"

I'm slightly taken aback by the tenderness in his voice and eyes, but I don't let it get to me. "There are many ways to take care of people, Lev. Ordering them around is not part of it."

"God" he groans, running his hands through his dark hair. "Why can't you just listen? This is for your own good." He peers at me through his long eyelashes. "You saw what happened last time you didn't listen to me."

For a solid second I find myself unable to say anything, shocked by his words. "You can't be serious right now."

"I most certainly am" he replies, not a hint of hesitation in his tone.

"You're not holding what happened against me" I murmur, my voice unsteady. "I know you're not."

His stare is grave and heavy on me. "It's the truth. I almost lost you because you didn't want to listen."

"I was barely scratched." I let out an incredulous laugh. "And it's not the point. I made a mistake, yes, but this doesn't mean I'm uncapable of deciding for myself."

"Coral—"

"No" I interrupt him, unwilling to listen to his foolishness. "No. You're not my father and I refuse to let you dictate my life. We're…" I wave my hands, struggling to find the right word. "We're dating, but that doesn't give you the right to tell me what to do."

Softness dusts his eyes, but I can still see the frustration hiding just beneath. "I want to protect you."

"You shouldn't be doing that" I reply in a small voice. "You should support me and be there for me, and you're amazing at it, but it isn't your job to protect me. See you when you stop being so controlling, Lev."

He tries to argue with my logic, but I don't give him the chance: I quickly grab my stuff and hop off the car, running to my apartment building.

I'm going to need some time.

CHAPTER TWENTY-FIVE

New York is pretty.

It's the end of November, so the city has already started to dress up in Christmas lights and decorations, and it feels magical to witness it in real life.

"It's huge." Sasha says, eyes scanning the Christmas tree in Rockefeller Center. "I thought it was all camera angles and optical illusions, but this is actually gigantic."

It is: the tree is majestic, with its size and the thousands of sparkly lights illuminating the cold night. I take a picture with my phone and start to send it to Lev, but at the last moment, I refrain. We're not on speaking terms, right now. Well, to be exact, I'm not on speaking terms with him—he's still trying to reach out, begging me to talk to him, to reconsider. I told him I'm not ending things, I just… I need some time. Things evolved so quickly between the two of us that I'm still trying to adjust, to understand the strong feelings I have for him, and if I actually want him to transform me. One thing's for sure: I don't want to spend the rest of eternity with someone who expects me to live under a glass bell, someone who thinks I'm in constant danger and that I need to be protected. Someone who wants to control me.

"Coral, hey." Piper clears her throat as she pushes a wool beanie over her big, fluffy curls. "Are you okay?"

I nod with way too much enthusiasm. "Yeah, sorry, lost in my thoughts. What's going on?"

"We were saying it would be nice to skate" she says, pointing at the big ice skating rink next to us. "Before we go grab some drinks. What do you think?"

"That's a great idea" I reply, plastering a big smile on my face. "Let's go!"

Piper and Sasha exchange a look I can't quite understand. They know something's going on with Lev, because they've seen me decline his calls and ignore his messages in the past few days, before we made it to NYC, but I haven't said a word about it. We're having this little trip to celebrate Piper's birthday and I don't want to ruin it with my whines.

Things seem to have calmed down, though: it's been a couple of days and Lev has stopped trying to contact me. I'm glad he's realizing I need some time alone to think and decompress, but at the same time… What if he changed his mind? What if it's him the one who doesn't want to be with me anymore?

"Man, I'm really looking forward to those drinks." Sasha snickers, wiggling her eyebrows in my direction. "You are too, you just don't know it yet."

I frown. "What do you mean?"

Before she can add anything else, Piper drags her away to buy the tickets, scolding her under her breath.

Oh, well. They've probably found out about my situation with Lev—I should've tried to be more subtle about it.

After purchasing the tickets and renting skates for the three of us, we finally enter the ice rink. We spend our time slipping and stumbling, clinging to each other to avoid disastrous falls, but most of all, we laugh.

"Sasha, you're literally an athlete" I wheeze, trying to balance myself with Sasha's dead weight holding onto my jacket's hood. "How comes you're so bad at this?"

"I'm a cheerleader!" she shouts, frantically moving her feet to try and stay afoot. "This has nothing to do with cheerleading, the ground is slippery!"

Piper is doubled over. "It's ice, of course it's slippery" she points out, before she starts howling with laughter again.

"Ohhh, I didn't realize you two were ice-skating world champions" Sasha snaps. "I can't..." But all this fuss makes her lose her balance once and for all: her right foot slides too far ahead, and she starts falling. Not before grabbing anything she can on her way down—my arm and Piper's coat being on top of the list.

We all tumble down on the freezing ice, a tangled mess of legs, wool scarves, and tiny squeaks.

Before we know it, we're losing it, sprawled on the world's most famous ice-skating rink, our laughter turning into clouds of steam in the cold night air.

God, my friends truly make everything better. I'm so glad to have them.

By the time we make it to the hotel bar where Piper insisted to go, despite it being far from our hostel, we're still delighted and giddy. And there's not even a drop of alcohol in our blood, at least not yet.

"Fancy" I say, looking around. The walls of the bar are covered in wooden panels, the mirrors on both ceiling and floor create dizzying but wonderful reflections, and the low, yellowish lights give the environment a mysterious vibe. The jazz music playing from speakers adds a special touch to it all.

We sit on the stools in front of the counter, where a nicely dressed bartender immediately gives us menus to pick a drink.

"Uhm" I murmur, looking down at my simple white turtleneck and high-waisted pants. "Guys, I think we don't exactly fit the dress code."

"It doesn't matter" Piper replies, a somewhat excited smile on her lips. "The most important thing is that we're here, isn't it?"

I nod in agreement, even though I'm not fully convinced.

"I didn't know you were into this kind of places."

"Oh, I saw this in a movie when I was a kid" she explains. "I've been wanting to come here ever since."

I nod again, but I notice the amused glance she and Sasha share. What are they not telling me?

Before I can voice my doubts, the bartender comes back to take our order. I'm not really into fancy, elegant drinks—plain vodka, beer, and cheap wine are my go to choice when it comes to alcohol—so I go with something safe, that I already know: a martini. I like olives, after all.

"Is there something wrong?" I ask, as soon as the bartender turns away to make our drinks. "I'm getting a weird vibe from you two."

Sasha and Piper look at each other for a split second, then their eyes dart back toward me. "No!" they both say at the same time, too nicely synchronized for it not to be suspicious.

"I'm not that dense, you know" I mutter, crossing my arms. "If you want to go do some sort of couple activity, it's okay, guys. Seriously." I put on a smile to try and convince them. "I'll find something to do in the meantime."

"It's not that." Piper gives Sasha a quick look, a glint of worry dancing in her dark eyes, then she glances back at me. "It's not. Trust me."

"Yeah, we have plenty of fun in the room when you fall asleep" Sasha chimes in, a mischievous smile on her lips. "Don't worry about it."

Piper's cheeks blush as she widens her eyes. "Sash, stop! It's embarrassing!"

She simply shrugs, drumming her fingers on the shiny countertop. "It's the truth."

"Then what is it?" I insist, holding back a laugh. "You're acting all weird, don't try to deny it."

Piper hesitates for a second, biting her lower lips, then she lets her shoulders drop down. "Alright. I guess we should give her at least a heads-up, right?"

"It would've been funnier without, but go ahead" Sasha sighs, just as the bartender comes back with our drinks. "Tell her. Ruin my fun."

"Tell me *what*?" I ask, grabbing my martini. I eat all the olives first, then I take a long sip of alcohol. Now that I know how these two spend their time once I fall asleep, I don't want to wake up by mistake and hear things I'm not supposed to hear.

"So." Piper clears her throat, looking at me through her lashes. "I told you how I was sorry for saying those things about Lev and judging him just because he's a... you know."

I nod, gulping down my drink. "Yeah, so?"

"So... He texted me right before we boarded the plane" she explains. "He told me about your fight, and that you wouldn't give him a chance to make things right."

"About that, it was kinda shitty of you to refuse that hotel upgrade." Sasha raises her pink and orange drink and takes a long sip through the glass straw. "Guy's filthy rich. Let him pay."

"It was a matter of principle" I reply, feeling my face grow warm. "I did it out of respect for Piper's mom, for the hard work she put in to afford this trip. It would've been an insult."

Piper clears her throat again. "Not really, but it's not the point." She stirs her virgin raspberry daiquiri with a straw. "I felt sorry about the whole situation and about the way I'd treated him, even though I did it indirectly, so I kind of agreed to help him out."

Just as I'm about to ask her to explain herself a bit better, a hand lightly brushes my shoulder, and I become aware of a warm presence standing behind me.

"And I'm more than grateful for it."

I squeeze my eyes shut, instantly recognizing that voice. Lev is here.

CHAPTER
TWENTY-SIX

I slowly turn around, and sure enough, here he is: standing right behind me, wearing a dark suit that fits him perfectly, his hair pushed away from his face. His expression is serious, but there's a certain tenderness softening his gaze.

"What are you doing here?" I ask, almost out of breath. I can't believe he's here.

"I need to talk to you." He lifts the corners of his mouth. "I apologize for inconveniencing the three of you on this lovely trip, but I couldn't wait any longer."

"Don't you have a… a business to run, back home?" I stutter. "People to meet? Money to make?"

He leans in, the scent of his aftershave fresh and minty around him. "You're more important."

I don't have a comeback for this. I simply stare at him, compulsively swallowing the excessive saliva in my mouth, my heart hammering in my chest.

"Come to my room with me?" he softly asks, tilting his head. "You don't have to stay, if you don't want to. I just want a quiet place to talk."

"She wants to stay" Sasha hurriedly says. "She most definitely wants to. It's not the best to have sex while she snores."

"Sasha!" Piper squeals, slapping her knee. "This is private!"

"About that." Lev pats his jacket and takes a white envelope out of an inside pocket. "To wish you a happy birthday, Piper, and to thank you and Sasha for all your help."

As soon as she opens it, her eyes widen. "We cannot accept it. You're very kind, but—"

"Of course we can accept it" Sasha interrupts her, snatching the envelope from her hands. "How very generous of you. We'll make sure to thoroughly enjoy it!"

"Babe, it's a week long trip to France for the both of us, plane tickets and all" Piper hisses.

I snap my head to look at Lev. "What?"

"You want to spend a week in France, too?" he murmurs. "Is that why you look so offended? Because I did not include you?"

"No, it's... No." I bite the inside of my cheek, flustered. "It's an expensive gift."

"And?" he asks, cocking an eyebrow. "You're scared I'm offending them?" He turns to face my friends. "Am I offending you, ladies?"

"Not in the slightest" Sasha reassures him. "We gladly accept your gift, right, Piper?"

Piper looks torn. "You're not offending us. It's just... It's an expensive gift, and there's no need—"

"There is" Sasha interrupts her. "Thank you, my guy. I'm so glad Coral decided to give you a chance."

"Me, too." His eyes are soft on me. "I hope I didn't blow it."

I'm so baffled by his presence here I don't have the presence of mind to answer, so I simply stare at him, unspeaking. Did he really come all the way to New York just to talk to me? And the fact that my friends were in on it...

I turn to them, slightly shaking my head. "We kind of need to talk."

"Yeah, not tonight." Sasha gets up from her stool and pats me on my back, a sly grin stretching her lips. "Tonight we all get to have some fun in peace. Don't try to come back to our room because I'm not opening the door."

"But I am" Piper says, giving her girlfriend a warning look. "Don't listen to her. If you need to come back, by all means, do it. Okay?"

Sasha wraps an arm around Piper's shoulders, wiggling her eyebrows. "Alright, but you might stumble upon something that—"

"Call if you need anything" Piper interrupts her. She leans in to place a kiss on my cheek, then gives Lev a stern look. "Don't harm her or we're going to have a problem."

"I'm not planning on it." He grins, watching Sasha drag Piper away, then he reaches down to whisper something in my ear. "If tonight I manage to make you scream, it's going to be for wildly different reasons."

CHAPTER TWENTY-SEVEN

When we make it to Lev's suite, his words are still ringing in my ears, a promise that's making my heart race in my chest. I keep telling myself I'm here to talk and to talk only, but there's a part of me that's more than willing to have his hands on me, to feel his body heat, to taste his cock in my m—

I stop myself mid-thought, and I can sense my face get warmer. Jesus. What is he doing to me?

"Nice room" I say, after clearing my throat. "Big. Fancy."

I might be trying to distract myself from my inappropriate thoughts, but I'm not lying: this place looks like an apartment you see on those glossy magazines nobody actually reads. There's a living room with a huge flat-screen hanging on the wall, cream and red armchairs, a thick rug on the floor, and a whole chandelier dangling from the ceiling. I can also see a corner of bedroom from the arched opening on the left.

"Glad you like it" Lev says, as he opens the minifridge. "Something to drink?"

I let myself fall down on the upholstered armchair, arching an eyebrow. "Are you trying to get me drunk?"

"Quite the contrary" he replies, then curves his mouth into a half-smile. "Intoxication hinders the conversation, and I wouldn't want you to forgive me too easily. I need to rightfully earn my absolution up to the last crumb." He points at the neatly lined bottles in the fridge. "I was about to offer orange juice."

I fight hard to hold back a smile of my own, but ultimately fail. "I'm okay, thanks."

"Let me know if you change your mind." He closes the fridge and comes to sit in front of me, his eyes closely searching mine. "I apologize for ambushing you here. Are you mad?"

I shrug, resisting the urge to look down. "I guess I'm mostly surprised. I thought... You weren't reaching out to me anymore, so I thought you had given up."

"On you?" He puts on an amused, softened smile. "I would never, baby. I hope you know that."

My heart drums, its pace quickening to the point I can almost hear the beating in my ears. "Now I know" I say quietly. "Why are you here?"

Lev takes his time before giving me an answer. He slowly loosens his dark tie, then he undoes the buttons of his cuffs, rolling up the sleeves of the shirt. His eyes don't leave mine, not even for an instant.

"I wanted to talk to you" he finally says, his voice deep and husky. "Apologize for my behavior."

I swallow, straightening my back. "Okay, go ahead. I'm listening."

"I'm sorry for the way I acted." He leans in, elbows planted on his knees, chin resting on his interwoven fingers. He's looking at me through his dark, long lashes. "You were right. I cannot decide for you, even if it gives me the illusion of keeping you safe." He slightly tilts his head. "I was speaking from a place of concern, and I did not realize that I was forcing my solutions upon you. I did not realize I was trying to exercise control and limit your freedom."

I slowly not, taking a deep breath. It's nice to hear it.

"I don't want to act like that scumbag of your ex-boyfriend" he goes on, a flicker of rage crossing his gaze. "I won't. It's not easy to suppress my instincts, but I can promise you, from now on I will try my best." He pauses, a hint of hesitation in his silence. "I will, if you give me the chance."

It's up to me, now. I can tell by the expectation burning like a fire in his dark eyes.

"There's a few things that I want to make clear" I say, biting my lower lip. "For this… For this relationship to work. I think it's important."

"Whatever you want." He nods. "Tell me everything."

I take a long breath, drumming on my knees with the tips of my fingers. "First, I want you to let me pay for my things. I can accept a gift every once in a while, but you need to remember that I'm a grown adult." I wet my lips, squirming under his intense stare. "Second, you'll stop sending me the money of our contract, since it's not valid anymore."

"Do I get a say in this?" he says, his voice calm, low.

"You can express your opinion, but these requests are kind of non-negotiable."

He nods, a pensive look on his face. "I get it. I still crave your blood, though. Don't you think it's fair for you to receive compensation?"

"No" I reply without hesitation. "I have feelings for you, now. It doesn't feel right to get paid to do something that… that I'd do anyway."

A sly grin appears on his lips. "I see. Good to know."

I give him a quick nod, ignoring how my heart is hammering in my chest. "Good. Third, I want you to respect my job, whatever it may be."

"Does this mean you're planning on switching jobs?"

I shrug, fighting the urge to smile. The satisfied glint shining in his eyes makes want to both slap and kiss him. "If I find something better, I will."

"Something better like your own bookstore?" he suggests. "I could make that happen, baby. I could fund it for you."

My half-smile falls in less than a second. "See? That's exactly what I'm talking about. I can make it on my own, but it feels like you don't believe it."

He opens his mouth, but slowly closes it again, seemingly taking my words in. Finally, he lets out a long sigh. "I apologize. It's not what I meant at all, but I can see why my words upset you." He straightens his back, his stare on me a bit frustrated. "But how can I support your dreams, then?"

"Listen to me when I talk about this stuff" I reply, tilting my head. "At least pretend to be interested in what I have to say."

"I wouldn't pretend" he replies, his voice soft. "I never will. Your dreams and aspiration are mine as well, if it's okay with you."

I nod, a small smile forming on my lips. He still has a long way to go, but I'm not perfect myself. I think... I think we can make this work, if we both put in the effort.

"What is the verdict?" His tone is amused, but there's a trace of concern nestled in his words. "Do I get your forgiveness?"

I get up from the armchair and walk toward him, my gait intentionally slow. "I don't know" I mutter, tilting my head to the side. "Maybe. Maybe not." I use his shoulders to balance myself as I sit on his lap, straddling him, then I lower my head to whisper in his ear, "You tell me."

His warm body stiffens under me. "Coral... What are you doing?"

"Actions speak louder than words, don't they?" I kiss his contracted jaw, then the tender flesh just beneath it. "I'm showing you just how much you're forgiven, if you want it too." I stop kissing him, my mouth hovering just inches from his scorching hot skin. "Do you?"

For a solid second, he simply stares at me from up close, his eyes pools of liquid darkness I wouldn't mind falling into. His breath is a soft, warm touch on my skin.

"Are you really asking?" he breathes, as his fingers slowly tap on my lower back. "Isn't my answer obvious?"

I straighten up, letting my nose brush his. "Hadn't we

already established that consent is crucial?"

"We had" he replies, his tone so low I can feel his words vibrate against my chest.

"So?" I murmur, slowly adjusting on his lap, careful to avoid the evident bulge in his crotch area. "Do you want it?"

"I've never wanted anything so bad in my entire life."

A split second and his mouth is on mine, demanding a kiss that was long overdue. Hot breaths mix and teeth collide and tongues explore, while his big hands settle on my ass, digging deep into the flesh.

"I missed you" I pant, letting myself sink into his lap, lightly rolling my hips. His cock is hard between my legs, the friction heavenly for my needy, pulsating pussy. "I missed you so much."

"Not as much as I missed you" he groans, pulling me even closer. "I want you on the bed. Can I take you? Please?"

"Yes" I whisper, wrapping my arms around his neck, holding tight as he gets up from the armchair.

Lev doesn't stop kissing me as he makes his way to the bedroom, stumbling on furniture and rugs and wall frames— he only pauses to gently put me down on the bed, the beige duvet soft under me.

"Tell me" he murmurs, crawling over me, his hands playing with the hem of my pants. "What do you want?"

I trace the line of the buttons keeping his shirt closed, letting my hand linger only inches away from his lower abdomen. "I want you to fuck me" I whisper, arching my back so that our chests brush together. "I want to come with your cock buried deep inside me, and I want you to suck my blood while I ride you. Is that okay?"

"Fuck." He takes my turtleneck off, throwing it across the room, and possessively kisses my neck. "You're killing me."

"So much for being the dangerous one" I murmur, as I undo the buttons of his shirt. His chest is solid and hot beneath my fingertips, a clear invitation to touch it. "It's good seeing you at my mercy. I like it."

He unclasps my bra, helped by my arched back, and cups my breasts with a firm and yet soft grip. "What about this?" He lowers his head, taking my left nipple in his hot mouth. He nibbles at it, sending a spark of electricity down my back. "Do you like this?"

I whimper my approval, snapping my eyes shut as he slowly licks and sucks my nipple, the feeling so intense I'm scared I'll pass out.

"Yes, you do" he coos, while pulling down my pants little by little. His fingertips brush the skin of my inner thighs and groin, leaving behind a trail of goosebumps. "You like my touch. You like my tongue on you."

I squirm under him in anticipation. My pussy is throbbing, and I can tell he knows—he knows damn well what he's doing to me, and he's enjoying every second of it.

"Please" I whine, reaching out to take his cock out of his pants. "Lev, please."

Before I can touch him, he grabs both of my wrists and pushes me back onto the mattress. "If you touch me now, I won't last long" he mutters, pinning my hands down. He playfully bites my left boob, only slightly grazing the sensitive skin before licking it with his raspy tongue. "I want your first time to be good. Unforgettable."

I want to tell him it will be no matter what, because it's happening with him, but the words die on the tip of my tongue when he presses a flattened palm against my pussy.

"You're already wet" he breathes, hooking his fingers underneath my panties to slide them off. "Your pretty cunt is drenched. Is that the effect I have on you?"

I can't answer his question: his thumb finds my clit, applying a delicious pressure on it, and my mind goes blank for a moment.

"You're so responsive to my touch" Lev says, as he starts rubbing where I'm most sensitive. "I'm about to slide a finger inside of you." His voice is calm as he explains what he wants to do to me. "You stop me whenever you want, baby.

Is that clear?"

"Yes." I nod, even if I doubt I'll ask him to stop. I'm dying to feel him push his cock inside me, so a finger is a small thing, in comparison. "Clear. Go on."

He doesn't stop rubbing my clitoris as his forefinger slowly slides in, making its way in my tight canal.

"Is this okay?" he asks. "Does it hurt?"

"Not at all." I push my hips up to get closer to him. "Lev, please. Please."

In the semi-darkness of the room, his smile glints mischievously. "Please what?" A second finger joins the first one, my pussy clenching and throbbing around them. "Use your words."

I can't: the way he's sliding his fingers in and out, while his thumb draws circles around my clit, is fogging up my mind. I couldn't tell left from right, at the moment.

"Fuck me" I manage, my voice barely above a raspy whisper. "Please, fuck me."

He doesn't make me ask a third time: he gets rid of his pants and underwear, letting his cock stand erect against his toned stomach. "We can stop whenever you want, yeah?" he murmurs, crawling over me. "You just say the word and we'll stop. You call the shots."

I pull him close to kiss him, pushing my hips toward him. "Fuck me, Lev. Fuck me senseless."

His cock rubs against my pussy a couple of times before it starts sliding in, one inch at a time.

"Fucking hell" he moans on my neck, his breath a hot caress. "You're so tight."

"Deeper" I beg, arching my back. "Push it in deeper."

He complies: he thrusts his cock deeper, deeper, deeper, stretching my pussy open, forcing me to close my eyes because it's all too intense. But not too painful, no. As I lie on my back, I take in the feeling of his hot dick filling me up to the last inch of space, almost splitting me open, but I find no pain—it's simply an intense, earth-shattering feeling.

181

"It's okay" I reassure him, caressing his back, kissing his jaw. "Go ahead, start moving. It doesn't hurt."

He doesn't make me beg: with a low moan, he does exactly what I asked, sliding in and out with an agonizingly slow pace, his mouth leaving kisses along my throat. His fingers find my clit and start stroking it, the pleasure so sudden and intense I roll my eyes back.

"Yeah" I whimper, rocking my hips to try and quicken our pace. "Like that. Faster, please."

"You feel so perfect" Lev groans, biting my lower lip. "Such a good girl, aren't you?"

A particularly strong thrust rips a cry from my throat. "Yes, yes, yes" I moan, almost desperately. This is out of this world—something I thought I'd never experience in my lifetime, and yet here I am.

Lev suddenly sits up and drags me with him, making me straddle his lap. His cock pushes deeper inside of me, and my clit deliciously rubs against his pelvis bone. The pressure is so intense I need to take a second to adjust, holding onto his broad shoulders for stability.

"I want to bite you" he says, hot breath caressing my neck. "To sink my fangs in your throat while I'm buried inside your dripping cunt."

"Please do" I whimper, my eyes still shut. "*Please*, Lev."

He licks the tender skin where neck and shoulder meet, places a kiss on it, then pierces it with his sharp teeth. His mouth sucks hard, greedily drinking my blood—it rips a desperate moan from me.

I sink my nails in his bare back, scratching him, pulling him closer, as I rock my hips in quick circles. The orgasm is building fast inside me, my pussy throbbing with anticipation.

"Fuck" I pant, rolling my head back, giving him better access to my throat. "I'm close."

He sucks and sucks, insatiable, his hands firmly gripping my ass, pulling me even closer. "You're a goddess" he murmurs, his voice wet and muffled with my blood.

This is enough to send me over the edge. One last hip roll and the pleasure explodes all at once, spreading in pulsating waves that make me cry and whimper at the same time. My pussy contracts, squeezing Lev's cock—in the span of two seconds, he fills my pussy with his hot cum, his entire body spasming in pleasure against mine.

"Oh, fuck" I whine, riding the orgasm to the very end, enjoying up to the last second of it. "Fuck. That was good."

"That's the understatement of the millennium" Lev groans, before licking my wound clean. He kisses his way up my neck and finds my mouth with his, still tasting like my blood. It's so hot. "It was heavenly. The best fuck of my entire existence."

With his cock slowly softening inside me, I snuggle against his chest, hugging him tight. "I think I want you to turn me" I say in a small voice. "No, scratch that. I know I want it."

"It's the orgasm talking" he murmurs as he rests his back on the pillows, pulling me down with him. "Let's postpone this decision until you can think straight again, yeah?"

"I've never been more clear" I reply, lifting my head to look at him in the eye. "I want to be with you for as long as possible. I want to be with you forever, Lev."

He curves his lips into a smart grin. "The dick's that good, huh?"

"It is" I admit without shame. "But it's not just that. It's the way you care for me. The way you're willing to recognize your mistakes and change." I let my fingers tenderly graze his toned chest, adjusting my position so I'm sitting more comfortably on his lap. "How you remember small details about me, how you always tell the truth, no matter what."

He stares at me for a couple of seconds, quiet, his eyes carrying emotions so heavy I can almost feel them in my chest. "You need to remember the turning is irreversible. You won't be able to go back."

"I know" I murmur. "I want it that way. Do you want to turn me?"

He nods, his fingertips brushing my chest, shoulders, arms. "I do. Not tonight, though. We need to be better prepared than this."

"I can wait" I whisper, a small smile on my lips. "We have eternity, after all."

"We do." He mirrors my smile and wraps his arms around my waist, pulling me against his chest. "And I can't wait to spend it all with you."

THE END

Printed in Great Britain
by Amazon